ISLAND OF THE LOST
A NEVERLAND NOVEL
BOOK III

BAILEY BLACK

BAILEY'S OTHER BOOKS

Fantasy Novels

The Lost Darling

Second Star to the Right

The Island of the Lost

The Cerise

Lucky in Love

ROMANCE NOVELS UNDER THE NAME BAILEY B

Broken Love Series

1. Beautifully Broken

1.5 Paper Hearts

2. I Hate You, I Love You Part 1

3. I Love You, I Hate You Part 2

Stand Alones:

Unexpected

Falling for You

In Too Deep

A GIFT ♡ FOR YOU

Thank you so much for purchasing the paperback of Island of the Lost!

If you're like me, you probably like to read in the dark, which can be difficult if you don't have a light or you have a partner who is a grumpfish and doesn't like the light. I get around this problem with ebooks and as a thank you for your support, I'd like to offer you a FREE ebook download on my website.

Head over to my website www.baileyblackbooks.com, or scan the QR code and find the Ebook titled **Wednesday and Naverland Book 3**. This is the discreet ebook version of this novel.

Use the code **James** at checkout and your ebook will be emailed to you through bookfunnel.

Download Your Ebook

Prologue

I left this world brokenhearted.

With wounds held together by bandages and duct tape.

I was dying inside, trying to put the pieces of my life back together. Unsure of up from down. Dreading spending each night alone because the memories of my sister and my ex-boyfriend's betrayal haunted me.

It's funny how the cuts on my heart, that I thought would never heal, are barely scars now.

How time, as unreliable as it may be, can mend all wounds.

Well, most.

The pain I feel now runs deeper than anything I've ever felt. I live another life every time I close my eyes. I feel Wendy's love for Peter and James as if it were my own, blurring the lines of everything I know. But walking in her footsteps each night is better than existing in this purgatory because there I get to see Peter.

I get to touch him in their stolen moments.

I get to hear his voice whispering to me in the dark.

And I get to feel her guilt for loving one brother more than the other.

CHAPTER 1
Wednesday

It's been days.

Days of waiting and hoping for Pan to come back to me.

Days of having takeout delivered because I didn't want to miss the moment he returned.

Days that drag on, minutes feeling like hours, and he still hasn't come back to me.

I look at yesterday's pizza box, still sitting on the table with a half-eaten slice inside, a war wages inside of me. On one hand, I should eat something because I skipped breakfast. What little of the plain cheese slice I tried to eat last night is all I've had in the last twelve hours. On the other hand, my nerves are so shot, I've barely been able to keep anything down.

Is it worth it to eat if I know I'm just going to throw it up later?

I roll onto my side and hold Pan's pillow to my chest, wishing it was him. Wendy Darling's emotions have twisted with mine, pushing away the anger and fear I clung to while in Neverland. I shouldn't let her feelings consume me. I would be better off hating both Peter and Pan for turning my life upside down. I *should* be thanking them for bringing me back to the life I begged and plotted to return to.

Instead, I'm drowning in depression, missing a man I never wanted to love, and desperate to return to a world no one believes exists.

I hold the pillow tighter, fully understanding why Wendy Darling donned a pen name and twisted her stories into the beloved fairy tale. She would have been put in an insane asylum had she told her truths any other way.

I've wondered more than once if talking to someone about what I went through might help ease the pain of missing the other half of my soul. At the very least, it would help me sort through how I feel and what I want. I might even figure out how to separate all things Wendy from my everyday existence and only draw on her experiences when I'm ready.

But the only person who knows I'm not dead is my sister, Tyle, and she is the last person I want to see.

Her life is perfect.

I huff out a laugh that is swallowed by a sob. Of course, it is. Tyle got everything I wanted in life, right down to our childhood home, while I'm stuck pining over an impossibility.

I bury my face in what's left of Pan's scent. Thanks to my breath, the cotton smells more like stale pizza than him, but it still has a hint of earth and magic. Soon, though, even that will be gone.

And then I'll have nothing.

A new wave of sadness has me crying again. I've given up trying to control my tears, let alone stop them. Centuries of longing flow through me, and every time I close my eyes, I let in a little more pain. Watching Wendy live her life, feeling it as if I'm experiencing it all myself, is torture. Yet, I willingly put myself through that pain because living in her reality while I dream is better than existing on my own.

A *rap, rap, rapping* on the door has my heart skipping a beat. No one should be knocking. I have the *do not disturb* sign on the door specifically to avoid human contact, and there isn't a soul alive who knows where I am.

Except for my Peter Pan.

Oh my gosh!

I wipe my eyes, excited and hopeful that Pan has returned. Or maybe it's Peter. I don't know who I want to see more. They're the same man, yet different all at once. Pan will likely barge into the room and take me in a hungry kiss. Peter will probably tuck his hands into his pockets and give me that lazy grin of his. Both will have me on my back within minutes of returning, and while I'd rather see them at the same time, having either one would send me over the moon. I love them both separately and equally and would be happy to see either.

But if I had to choose...

Hell, I'm not sure I could.

I run my fingers through my hair and try to make myself look somewhat decent. I should have taken a shower and I'm kicking myself for not thinking to be ready for when the other half of my soul returned, but there's no time now.

I hurry to the sink, put on some deodorant, then brush my teeth for all of thirty seconds. My mouth feels cleaner and minty, and while I'm too gross for sex (I need to shave pretty much every inch of my body), I don't feel like a cavewoman anymore.

He knocks again.

"I'm coming!" I yell. My heart races with each step and my stomach lurches. I'm so excited I could puke, but I try to hold it back. That would ruin our reunion. Although even if I did, we'd probably laugh about it later.

A small arrow of fear strikes my bubble of excitement because three days is just a few hours in Neverland. I doubt Peter has found Cass yet, but if he's here, that means one of two things. Something terrible has happened or it's safe enough for me to return.

I'm praying it's the latter because being in this world again is torture. Time moves too slow, forcing me to feel more than I ever thought possible.

I reach for the chain on the door. My fingers fumble, the connection between them and my brain broken, like a song on a fuzzy radio station. Bits of what I want them to do eventually break through the static and I finally slide the chain, twist the latch on the door, and tug it open.

My heart falls to the floor so hard that I have to bite my tongue until it bleeds to keep my tears at bay.

It's not him.

Of course, it's not.

"Thank God. You're here!" Tyle throws her arms around me and pulls me into a hug. She then cradles my cheeks in her hands, looking at me like she's scared I'll disappear the moment she closes her eyes.

"How did you find me?"

Tyle drops her hands and we awkwardly stand in the hallway until it hits me that she's waiting to be invited in. I step to the side and open the door wider. Her nose wrinkles once she's inside. I sniff the air. It has a mild sour smell, so I don't judge her for the face she makes, even though I know she's judging more than just the room.

"Someone left a note a few days ago stating you were here, in this room, and to come get you." She lifts the pizza lid. A fly scurries out, and I'm glad I decided to skip lunch. "I thought it was a joke. Kenny had told Kierra that you'd come back the other day, she went to a dark place after you died, and I thought the note might have been her way of coping with an old wound. But it was eating at me. So, I came." She pokes her head into the bathroom and relaxes when she realizes it's empty. "Where is Peter?"

"You remember his name?" I ask, surprised. Tyle used to go through boys so quickly that she'd name them all *handsome* so she wouldn't call her new toy by the old toy's name. The fact that Peter's name stuck after knowing him for less than ten minutes is shy of a miracle.

"How could I forget? Peter has haunted me ever since I met him. It took me a minute to match his face when I saw him at the house, but there was no mistaking who he was once I did." She lets the part about him being the man who took me hang in the air. I don't finish the statement for her and desperately hope she doesn't ask.

"He left," I say as impassively as possible. She won't understand that every minute he's gone, I die a little inside. Hell, I don't even fully understand. All I know is that I feel like a ghost in this world without my Peter Pan.

Tyle takes a hard look at me and frowns. "You're sad about that?"

I shrug, not having a good explanation. "It's complicated. You wouldn't understand."

"I understand perfectly, Wednesday. It's called Stockholm syndrome. You were held captive by him for years and you fell in love. It's perfectly normal, but that doesn't make it okay." She reaches out and touches my arm. "I can help you through this."

I jerk free of her touch, horrified. She doesn't know anything. Peter Pan didn't hold me prisoner. He was my friend. He saved me more times than any man should need to. She's wrong! "I don't need help, Tyle. I'm fine."

I turn my back to her, walk back to the bed, fall into the heap of blankets, and grab Pan's pillow again. I close my eyes and wish for sleep, desperate to see Peter's face again.

"This place is a dump, Wens." Tyle tries to shift the conversation, and that tone, the one laced with judgment and disappointment, comes out of hiding.

"Why are you here, Tyle?" I don't look at her. I don't want to see her glowing with love as she grows her baby. Yes, I'm still bitter. Just because I don't love my ex—or want him anymore—doesn't mean I can't still be angry.

Family is supposed to be forever.

They are supposed to be the people you can always count on.

My family isn't in this room. They're back in Neverland because those people are more loyal to me than my own blood.

"I was worried about you." The bed dips as Tyle sits beside me. She pushes the blankets back until I have no choice but to look at her. Dark bags peek through her concealer. She looks tired and years older as her makeup folds into the fine lines of her face. "When that man took you again..." She bites her lip and shakes her head. "I thought I'd lost you."

"Stop." I push up onto one arm and glare at my sister. "Stop pretending that you care about me. You don't. You haven't since the seventh grade when you woke up and decided that we weren't twins anymore."

"Wednesday." Tyle swallows hard and closes her eyes. I give her a minute, although I'm unsure why, and wait for her to compose herself again. "I'm sorry."

"Sorry can't change the past." I get up and start cleaning my mess because I don't know what else to do. I can't just sit here and pretend that singular word erases years of trauma, because it doesn't.

"I know." She sighs, taking the empty bag of chips from my hand and carelessly dropping it to the floor. "But damn it, Wednesday, you're all I have. We have to stick together."

"What about Kenny?" I raise my eyebrows, curious about her response.

"Things with Kenny are complicated. We got married because of Wanda, but we don't love each other. He's been cheating on me since before the wedding." Tyle drops into the chair, unconcerned about crushing my only clothes.

"Sucks, doesn't it?" I cross my arms, wanting to hold on to my anger, but as I watch my sister wither from the strong woman who didn't care about anyone but herself to a broken shell of that person, I can't stay mad.

"You know what they say." She forces a smile and tries to sound playful, but I can hear the tears on the brink of breaking free. "What goes around comes around." She sniffles and then stretches her smile wider. "Enough about me. What are you doing, Wednesday? Why are you in this hellhole? This place reeks, and, no offense, you look like shit."

The look Tyle gives me warms my heart because if Mom could see her, she'd be proud. Tyle has mastered the *I'm disappointed but still love you* face.

I'm not sure what to say. Outside of what I did a few minutes ago, I haven't made any effort to brush my hair, put on makeup, or even find matching clothes since Pan left. All I've done is sit here and cry.

And wait and cry.

And eat and cry.

And then throw up because I'm so upset and anxious and ready for him to come back that I can't keep anything down.

But if Tyle is here because Pan sent her, I can't help but fear he knew that he'd be gone more than a few days. The color drains from my face when it hits me that he may never return. Pan planned for my sister to find me because he knew I wouldn't leave this room. Ten lifetimes of money sits in his account and I would have spent half of it wasting the years away.

Just. Waiting.

The shred of hope I have that he'll return shatters. I bury my face in his pillow again, overwhelmed with a new round of tears. Tyle shifts and holds me in her arms. She can't begin to understand my pain, and still, she keeps me in her embrace, trying to ease the ache.

"Wednesday." Her voice cracks as she fights her own wave of emotion. "Come home."

"I don't have a home."

"Yes, you do. Your home is with Kenny and Wanda and me. We've missed you." She pulls back and looks me in the eyes. "We love you."

I lean against the side of the bed and curl my knees into my chest, wrapping my arms around them. I don't know if I can be in that house without Mom. It hurts too much.

Tyle sits beside me and touches my back. "It doesn't have to be forever," she adds, reading my mind. "Just until we get you settled, sort out the whole death certificate thing, and get a job. You're welcome to stay as long as you want, but I know you won't."

I laugh humorously at the thought of living with my sister and her husband. The three of us under the same roof, playing house, sounds like a nightmare.

"How have you been paying for this?" Tyle asks, looking around the room again.

"Peter left me some money." I pause, tempted to keep everything Peter and Pan related to myself, but I need help moving and probably selling the car. So, I add, "And a car."

"He gave you a car?" she asks, eyebrows arched.

I nod and laugh when I say, "I don't know how to drive it. It's a stick."

"Oh, honey, once you learn how to work a stick, it comes naturally," my sister says with too much enthusiasm, trying to cheer me up. She wiggles her eyebrows and I can't help but laugh with her. It feels so good not to be in constant competition with each other.

Neverland years aside, I can't remember the last time we sat together and got along without pretending.

"Please, Wednesday, even if it's just for a few days, you need to get out of this place. It smells like puke in here." She wrinkles her nose again.

That's because I can't keep anything down.

I let my head fall against the mattress and stare at the popcorn ceiling. As much as I don't want to be around Kenny or in that house, I don't want to be alone. Heartbreak is harder when you're alone. "I don't know."

"Okay. No pressure, we can talk about where you'll live later." She holds up her hands in mock surrender. "What about lunch then?"

"Huh?"

"Lunch. Let me take you to the mall. We'll go shopping and get something to eat. My treat."

I'm about to tell her no when my stomach cramps. I touch my belly, feeling its angry rumbles. I'm still not used to all the additives this world puts into its food. I throw up half of what I eat, which is why I've mostly had chips the last two days. Something about the grease and the salt mixes with me. It's the only thing I can keep down but I probably should put something besides crap in my stomach. And I really do need some more clothes.

"Fine," I concede. "Let me take a shower and get ready."

"Oh, thank God."

"What?"

"I didn't want to say anything, but you smell terrible." She grins, teasing and telling the truth all at once.

I grab a pillow that isn't Pan's and chuck it at Tyle as I pass the bed. I don't forget the years of bullshit she's put me through, or how I still hate her, but a small part of me is glad Tyle showed up.

With her here, I'm not alone.

CHAPTER 2
Wednesday

"Oh! Try this one on." Tyle tosses another pair of pants over the fitting room door.

I've gone up three sizes since Pan left.

I shouldn't be surprised. All I've done is lay around and let carbs cling to my hips, but it still stings. I know we're in that wave of life where all bodies are beautiful and skinny isn't the only way to be anymore, but I can't unprogram my grandmother's words from whispering in my ear.

Never above a size three. Sorry, Grams. I was a solid five before I left this world. Now, I'll be lucky if I can squeeze into an eight.

"Don't stress." Tyle tries to comfort me, but it's a hard pill to swallow. "I don't even look at the numbers anymore. Every designer is different, so they aren't universal. A seven in this store could be a four in the next."

I shimmy out of the jeans and tug my shorts back on. Even they feel tight today. I sigh, fold the pants I don't want, and rehang the shirts and dresses back on their original hangers. "I'm done."

"Are you sure?" Tyle asks when I open the door, holding two more flowing dresses draped over her arms. Neither of which looks like anything I would pick for myself. "We could try a different store."

I shake my head. "I don't want you spending any more money on me."

"I don't mind." Her eyes go wide as a new idea comes to mind. "I know! We can get our toes done. I haven't seen mine in—"

"Tyle!" I cut her off. Today has been great, but I've done more walking in the last three hours than I have since leaving Neverland. My feet are killing me and the veins in my hands are swelling. I have to wiggle my fingers to keep the skin from pulling too tight and hurting. "Thank you, but no. I'm ready to go."

"Where?" she asks, worry weighing heavily in her tone. "You can't go back to that ratty motel, Wednesday. You'll catch a disease."

"I'll figure it out."

"How? You don't have a job to pay for anything. Heck, according to the government, you're dead! Red flags will fly if you try to get a place and they have to run your social."

I hang the clothes I don't want on the return rack and grab my bags. Tyle's bought me five outfits: three dresses, a bathing suit, some pajamas, and a pair of flip-flops. A part of me feels bad. This is money she should be spending on the new baby and, if Peter's account is as flush as he described, I can more than pay for the things I need.

But I know the moment I say his name or mention anything that has to do with him, Tyle's sweet side will vanish. She'll either turn into a crazed mother-hen again or the switch will flip to bitch because I refuse to let her talk shit about him. It's easier to keep my secrets and enjoy this happy, loving side of my sister than it is to rock the boat.

"One night," I concede. "I'll give you one night, but I swear, Tyle, if Kenny does anything even remotely shady, I'm cutting his balls off."

She laughs, assuming I'm joking. "Relax. You have nothing to worry about. Kenny will behave."

"How do you know?"

"Because you're not his type anymore." Her smile falls for a fraction of a second, letting slip the hurt she tries to hide from the world, but then is back in place bigger and brighter than before.

I touch my chest and drop my jaw in fake despair. "I'm crushed. How ever will I survive?"

"The same way I've been." Tyle links her arm with mine and grins. "By eating your weight in ice cream every chance you get."

***

I clench my teeth and push the bowl of ice cream away. My stomach has tied itself into a ball of knots. Milk wasn't something we used in Neverland. I don't think I can handle the dairy anymore.

"What's wrong?" Tyle asks.

"I don't feel good." I lay my head on the cold countertop and ground myself to the sensation. It feels good against my clammy skin.

"Again? You didn't feel good after lunch either."

"The food wasn't so processed where I came from," I admit. We haven't gotten into the details of where I was. I think Tyle is afraid to ask, but she knows, at its core, I was in a different world. Except she thinks that phrase is a metaphor and not a hard truth.

"Please don't be mad, Wens," Tyle says hesitantly. She chews on her bottom lip, a habit we both have when nervous, and asks, "But, is there any chance you could be pregnant?"

"No," I say without hesitation and laugh. "Definitely not."

"It's just you're food sensitive and your clothes don't fit and if I'm being honest, your belly is a little distended."

"Believe me. It's not possible."

"When was your period?"

"I..." I try to remember, but it was before Neverland. About two weeks before we went to the Keys. Three years ago. How do I explain that? "I'm not sure. A few weeks ago, I guess. It's not like I could keep track of the days."

Tyle leaves the kitchen and walks down the hall, then comes back with a piss test in her hand. "Humor me."

"Why do you have that?"

"It's an extra from when we found out about Wyatt. After the second positive test, I didn't see the point in wasting any more." She grabs my shoulders and low-key lifts me off the barstool. "Go. If you just had it a few weeks ago, then there's nothing to worry about."

"Seriously, Tyle. This is stupid."

She sticks the test down my shirt, loosely tucking it between the girls. "Stupid or not, it will make me feel better."

It might make her feel better, but my insides are squirming. The likelihood of me being pregnant is less than one percent, but there's still a chance. One I'm not ready to confront. "You're not gonna let this go. Are you?"

"Nope."

"Fine." I groan and set off down the hall to the bathroom. Someone has fixed the sink. You'd never know Pan destroyed the room just a few days ago. I almost wonder if Kenny's face has healed, but then decide I don't care.

I prep myself to pee on the test and my heart foolishly races. If we were in the real world, I would be nervous. Between my boys and Cass, I've had enough semen inside me to get a nun pregnant by immaculate conception. But Cass said he couldn't get me knocked up. It's physically impossible. Both him and Peter's swimmers are dead, and by default, that means Pan's are too.

Plus, I have the implant in my arm.

My bladder relieves itself the moment I'm seated on the toilet and ready. Peeing on demand has never been a problem for me. The skill has come in handy more than once with the random drug tests my job used to do. Though I never would have thought it would be useful for something like this.

I cap the end of the stick and set it on the counter while I pull up my pants. I turn to flush and the blinking screen of the digital test catches my eyes. The world around me stills into one long moment. Disbelief has me questioning the validity of the test. I had the results in less than a minute. That and the test almost nine months old. It could be wrong.

It has to be wrong.

But as I read the results over and over again, I know it is right.

I'm pregnant.

CHAPTER 3
Wednesday

"Wens?" Tyle softly knocks on the door, her knuckles echoing through the silence. "Are you okay in there?"

I hug my knees to my chest and bury my face in my arms. I don't know how many minutes have passed. I've been in here long enough for my eyes to run out of tears and my heart to stop hurting, but not long enough to numb the ache of emptiness inside me.

The nurse in Fort Lauderdale knew I was pregnant.

That's what she was hesitant to tell me, and the only reason I can think of why that information would have been withheld is because Pan knew and had asked them not to say anything.

He knew I had a baby in my belly, and he still left.

"I'm fine," I manage to say, my voice trembling.

Tyle's tone is heavy with concern as she tries to coax me out of the bathroom, but I'm not going anywhere. "You don't sound fine, Wens. I'm coming in."

The door creeps open. Tyle pokes her head in first. I raise my bloodshot eyes over my arms and look at a speck of dirt on the tiles by her feet. She moves closer, her voice barely a whisper, "You are. Aren't you?"

I can't meet her gaze. Instead, I curl further into myself, hiding my face in my arms again. It's confirmation enough, but if Tyle needs more the test is still on the counter, happily blinking *Pregnant* for the world to see.

Tyle grunts and groans as she slides down the wall, but she manages to sit beside me on the floor. Her warm arms wrap around me, offering fragile, unexpected solace. We sit together, neither one of us saying anything as a new wave of tears runs its course. "Whatever you decide, Wens, I support you."

My throat feels raw, every syllable an effort to utter, but I manage to ask, "What?"

"There are options," she says as gently as she can, but her words hang heavy in the air. "You don't have to keep it."

I sit upright, disgusted that Tyle would suggest I give away my child. Peter's child. Or is it Pan's? Stars above, I hope it's not Cass's baby. All three of them came inside me within days of each other. Granted, it's been a few weeks since I slept with Cass, but I don't know where I was in my cycle when I fucked him.

I'm either growing a half-fairy or a zombie. I'd laugh if the prospect wasn't so depressing. I don't know what this child is or what it might be able to do and I am the only person in this world who could care for it.

Besides, if it were discovered that my baby could fly or freeze things or do any of the possible gifts it could get from its father, it would be studied and experimented on. Its life would be nothing but pokes and prods, blood draws and scans, and tests upon tests. I refuse to let that happen.

Gathering my strength, I raise my head and meet Tyle's gaze. She needs to understand, even if I can't put into words what I need to say. "I'm keeping it."

"Wednesday." She sighs. "Keeping the child of your kidnapper could be emotionally damaging."

"And giving it away would be worse." I look at my sister, silently begging her to understand without giving my reasons. I can't explain, but she's a mom. She has to understand how hard it would be to carry Wyatt for nine months and then never see him again.

"We're going to need a nanny to take care of all of these babies." She leans in and nudges me with her shoulder.

"Or a dog named Nanna," I tease. Tyle's brows knit together.

The reference went so far over her head that I don't even bother trying to explain. "Never mind."

Tyle tries to push herself to her feet, but her big belly gets in the way. I stand before she can roll onto her side with the intent of getting on her hands and knees, and offer her a helping hand. I stumble back a step at the awkwardness of her weight, and we both laugh.

"I'll need to sell Peter's car," I say, the heaviness of reality crashing down upon me.

Tyle's eyebrows shoot up in surprise. "That's right! I forgot he left you a car."

I nod. "And a little money. Not a lot," I lie, "but enough to get me on my feet again."

"Where is it? What is it?" Tyle whispers as we make our way back to the living room. She pokes her head into Wanda's room and peeks in at her. She smiles, reassured that her daughter is sleeping soundly, and closes the door again. "Do you have the title? Kenny can pick it up from... where is it?"

"The cemetery."

"Seriously? He left you at Mom and Dad's all alone!" Tyle shakes her head, her hatred for Peter growing with every new sentence I say. "I swear if I ever see that man again, I'm going to kill him."

I try to downplay the situation to reassure her. "It's fine, really." But deep down, the hurt of being abandoned in this world lingers like an open wound. "And I don't know about the title. Is there a way to see who he registered it to without raising any red flags?"

Tyle chews on her bottom lip and stares off into space for a minute. Her gaze snaps back to mine a second later, a mischievous grin dancing on her lips. "Maybe. I have a friend at a dealership who might be able to work some magic. I'll give him a call."

Tyle pushes off the couch and heads toward the kitchen where her phone is. I watch her hobble, wondering if I'll get that big or if this baby is going to grow faster having been conceived in Neverland. I set my hands on my belly and look down.

Peter was wrong. The greatest adventure of my life won't be dying. It will be raising our baby (I refuse to believe it could be Cass's).

I smile at my non-existent pudge, imagining what motherhood could be like when a cool breeze sweeps through the room, sending shivers down my spine. I reach for the blanket laid across the cushions behind me when I hear the softest whisper in my mind.

"Hello, Darling."

CHAPTER 4

Pan

Someone kicks me in the side, causing a sharp pain to ripple through my body. The ache lingers, refusing to fade away, despite the Island's usual reach to mend the broken.

Seconds pass and my magic doesn't heal me. It should have. Just like it should have called to the sky for rain and the ocean for waves. Yet, its power eludes me. I can feel the pulsating energy as it stirs beneath the earth, vibrating with an almost taunting presence. I can taste the metallicness in the air, but I can't make any of it listen to my pleas.

A voice slices through the silence, etching itself like a scar in my mind. "I thought the great Peter Panning would be more difficult to capture." I recognize it without needing to see the face to know whom it belongs to. Belle—Cass and Emmit's sister —kicks me in the side again and says, "Pity."

The rough burlap sack over my head is abruptly ripped away, revealing a dimly lit room. My eyes take a moment to adjust to the pale glow of fireflies in lanterns, but I recognize where I am as. I'm in a holding room deep within one of the caverns beneath the stone castle carved into the mountainside. One of the many forgotten dungeons the Fae King used to keep.

Peter's friends, the Lost—Aria, Heidi, Emmit, and Xyris— hang in iron shackles from their wrists alongside me, their unconscious forms swaying slightly. The only one awake is Emmit. His head moves in the slightest, warning me. I don't know what the warning is for, but whatever it is, I'm not supposed to do it.

"Tell me, Peter." Belle's voice echoes in the barren space

while her footsteps click ominously. She remains hidden in the dark, her presence felt rather than seen. "Are we going to do this the easy way or the hard way? I do so hope you make things difficult. I haven't had any fun in ages."

Belle finally steps into the dim light wearing a glittering green floor-length gown. The woman looks ready for a ball, not a torture session, but that is Belle. Her vanity is her greatest weakness, aside from her hunger.

I force a grin and try my hardest to sound like my other half. It's been so long since Peter has seen Belle. I doubt she'll notice the difference between my eyes and his, but she'll recognize my voice. I sound too much like James.

I was cursed with the parts of Peter that he didn't want, including anything that tied him to his old life. Like his accent. And most of his memories. "Good to see you, Belle. You don't look a day over two hundred."

Belle studies me. I've only had a voice for a few days. Trying to hide my natural accent is difficult but not impossible. *But do I sound like Peter?*

Her lack of response makes me nervous. I blow Belle a kiss and her nose wrinkles. She looks at me like I'm a dog who just shit on her shoes and then dragged all of my crap on the train of her dress. She schools her face to seem impassive, but I can see the rage pooling beneath the surface. Good. That's something I can work with.

"Where's the girl?" Belle demands, her tone laced with impatience. I feel a small sense of relief, but I don't let it linger. I'm on a ticking time bomb, the fuse growing shorter the longer we're in each other's presence. My only hope is that Belle's lack of patience will make her careless.

"You have a room full of pretty girls. Which one would you prefer?" I reply, feigning innocence. There is only one woman worthy of Belle's time, The Darling, and she will never have her.

With a swift motion, Belle's open hand lands a stinging slap across my face. "Please play games with me, Peter," she says, fury bleeding into her sarcasm. "I want so badly to make you bleed."

I press my lips together and swallow a knot of nervousness. My heart ticks faster. The moment she tastes my blood, she'll know I'm not Peter. She will drain me, mercilessly, for the mere pleasure of it and absorb what's left of my magic into her veins.

But that's not the worst part. When a Fae drinks the blood of another, they gain access to their memories, though it's the last drop that holds a person's greatest secret. Belle would bleed me dry for that drop alone because it would lead her to Wednesday.

I can't let that happen.

"Do it, Belle. I dare you," I challenge, my voice trembling slightly. "Cut my skin. Taste my flesh because without my shadow it will be ash in your mouth. It will take back every year you've stolen and you'll be nothing but dust in the wind."

"Liar!" she screams. She grips my chin between her fingers and tries to compel me into telling the truth, but she's weak. Her magic wraps around my words, but they aren't strong enough to rip them from my lips.

I bite down on my tongue until I taste iron, then lick my lips, purposely staining them red. I pray she doesn't call my bluff, but this is something Peter would do. "Want to find out?"

Belle huffs in frustration and shoves my forehead. My skull cracks against the stone. Pain—a feeling I'm not used to and have only felt secondhand—wraps around my head and shoots down my spine. It's intense and dizzying, but I laugh because that's what Peter would do, too. He'd poke the bear over and over until she lost her temper. Before the Darling arrived, every-thing was a game to him.

One he always had to win.

"Your blood may be no good to me, but I have a buffet of souls to choose from. Where should I start, Peter?" Belle walks past our friends, dragging her nails across each one's cheek, spilling blood as she makes a turn around the room. "Which pathetic little half-mortal do you love most?"

"Leave them alone, Tinkerbell!" Emmit roars. He pulls against the iron cuff. The metal sizzles as it sears another layer of his skin away. I know it hurts, it has to, but Emmit hides the pain behind a mask of indifference. "They aren't a part of this."

"Sweet baby brother," she coos, her words laced with false affection as she turns her attention to him. "Don't you understand? I'm doing all this for us."

"Liar!" he growls. "You've only ever thought about yourself. This has nothing to do with me."

"Do you know what our father had planned for you? He was going to ship you off to war. He wanted you dead." She touches her chest, giving an Emmy-worthy show of practiced care that he sees straight through. "I saved you."

"You killed him. You killed everyone."

"I did it for you," Belle claims. Her voice cracks and I might've believed her if I didn't know better. But I do know better. Just like I know about the souls she bleeds to feed her thirst and how the more vital the memory, the stronger her magic is. I know that her borrowed power lasts days, sometimes less, before it wanes and she's forced to feed again.

"You killed them to be queen. You don't care about me. You never have," Emmit counters, a vicious smirk curling his lips. "Too bad the Island saw through your bullshit and picked someone else to rule."

Belle smacks him and her nail slashes across his cheek, leaving a deep gash that seeps crimson. "Now look what you've made me do," she mutters, a mixture of irritation and disappointment clouding her face. Belle heaves a sigh and strides over to Heidi, unchaining her and dragging her by the wrist toward Emmit. "Drink," she commands. "Once you taste the power their memories hold, you'll be so much stronger."

"No."

Belle cuts Heidi's wrist with her thumbnail. Blood wells up

and leaks down her pale skin. "Your body won't heal itself without help anymore. Drink!"

"No!"

"Why not?" Belle demands.

"Because she's my friend," Emmit says defiantly. "I won't do it. I won't be like you."

"Put her life to use or waste it. I don't care. Either way, she dies," Belle coldly retorts. She slides her thumbnail across Heidi's neck, slitting the artery that feeds the brain, then drops the body. Blood leaks out of our friend at an inhuman speed, a puddle of deep red stains the dirt and seeps into her clothes.

"Stop this, Belle! Stop her bleeding," Emmit pleads, desperation creeping into his voice. He pulls at the cuffs again. They've rubbed his skin raw, down to the muscle. If he doesn't stop, they'll eat through his hand.

Belle pretends to consider for a moment, feigning kindness. She shakes her shoulders and a shower of golden dust fills the air. She catches a handful of it and tosses it at Emmit. He stops writhing, his body frozen in place, save for the movement of his eyes.

"I think I'd rather have you watch her die," she remarks, a sinister edge to her voice. "All you had to do was take one little taste. You could have healed her the moment your strength returned, but you chose to let her rot. What happens next is on you."

She steps forward and cups his cheeks in her hands, ducking down to meet him at eye level. "I am not your enemy, little brother. One day, you'll see that."

Belle's attention shifts back to me. "As for you," she declares. She walks to each of the Lost and tosses her golden dust on them, ensuring that time cannot touch their motionless forms. "Every day you delay, another one of your friends will die." She stands before me, her gaze locking with mine.

I clench my teeth, refusing to break eye contact. We've

found ourselves in another game, one I'd happily lose to kick her in the stomach if I weren't pretending to be someone else.

Now would be a good time to come back, Peter. My thoughts are torn between chastising him for abandoning us and all the ways I'm going to kill this bitch when I get free.

"I will drain every last drop of their blood. I will extract their souls, and I will obliterate any chance of them having a life beyond this one," Belle threatens, a wicked smile playing on her lips. "I've been generous by allowing you to keep your pets." She pauses and smirks. "Did you think I didn't know? I know everything, Peter. I've kept my word to your brother all these years, but the Darling changes everything."

"What did my brother promise you?"

"You have... seven friends, correct?" Belle's voice drips with malice. "Will you let them all die? Or perhaps just this one? The choice, Peter, is yours."

"Belle!" I shout, my voice filled with a mixture of desperation and defiance. "What deal did James make?"

She chuckles wickedly and turns the corner, leaving me alone with nothing but my thoughts.

CHAPTER 5

James

"What are you going to tell her?" Smee asks, her voice laden with worry. She nervously twists the tassel on her shirt, wrapping it around her finger repeatedly. "It's been almost a week and there haven't been any new souls in the Neversea. That's never happened."

"I know." We've combed the dark blue waters for hours this morning, searching for even one soul passing through. There weren't any. Just like there weren't any the day before. Or the one before that. If I'm counting correctly, there hasn't been a new soul since Peter left with the Darling girl. A fact that hasn't stopped rolling around my mind since she left.

"Belle could start feeding off us again."

"I know."

"I don't want to give her another piece of me, Cap," Smee continues, her voice trembling. Fear and sorrow mingle in her words, while panic pushes its way to the forefront of her emotions. "I can't let her feed on me again. We can't give her the others, either. She's—"

"Smee!" I yell, and my voice reverberates in the ship's cabin.

She flinches. I pinch the bridge of my nose and close my eyes. Raising my voice was a mistake I already regret, but I had no choice. I know Smee's traumas and make a conscious effort to avoid triggering her. Yet, today, I've failed.

Releasing a deep breath, I look at my friend. Smee tries her best to hold herself together, but her resolve is crumbling. Her pain is my fault, a weight that does not sit easy on my chest. I step forward and pull her into my arms. "I'm sorry."

Smee nestles her face against my chest, her breathing uneven and ragged. She hates crying. Another trauma from another life she's lived. Pain is funny like that. It scars the soul in ways the living can't imagine and resurfaces whenever it pleases.

"I promise," I assure her, my voice steady. "Nothing is going to happen to yeh."

She looks up at me, her eyes reddened by tears she doesn't want to shed. "What about the others, Cap?"

I cup her cheeks and press my forehead to hers. Neverland is the bridge between life and death, and my ship has become the Ferry that takes souls to the afterlife. Most willingly embark on the journey, content with the lives they've lived and ready forf the afterlife, but every so often I find a soul who is tormented and not ready to move on.

I offer them a chance to work through their demons and a safe space where they have all the time in the world to process whatever is holding them back from transitioning into the afterlife.

For a cost.

A memory.

One they have no say in losing.

I don't reveal the full extent of the consequences or how painful it is to let go of something that defines their very being. Or the agony they'll endure when Belle sinks her teeth into them to extract it. But I do promise it will only happen once.

A promise I will do anything to keep.

I brush away the long strands of auburn hair that have fallen over Smee's eyes. "She won't touch them. I'll take care of it."

"How?"

Her doubt is unnerving, but I try to reassure her. I recognized long ago that this woman was going to be the metaphorical death of me. Her smart mouth. Those pretty brown eyes. That unwavering trust and dedication. She offered me something no one in my life ever had, true dedication. So, I made her my first mate.

"I'm scared, Cap." She tugs at the lapels of my coat, trying to get closer, but there's barely enough room for the air between us.

I force myself to remain patient and not patronizing. I remember what it felt like to be afraid. The sensation was lost to me until the other day when I saw Wednesday unconscious in Peter's arms.

Watching him fly away with her damn near broke me, but I had to let them go. Getting her out of Neverland was the only thing that could save her but that doesn't mean a single day hasn't gone by where I haven't lost sleep, wondering if she's okay.

"Do yeh trust me?" I arch back and duck to find Smee's eyes.

She nods, her conviction clear. "With my life."

"Good." I kiss her hairline and step away. The sun is nearly at its peak in the sky. I can't stay much longer or I'll be late. Belle hates it when I'm late. I grab my sword off the center table and my hat from the hook. "I'll be back."

"Where are you going?" Smee follows me to the deck but doesn't cross the ramp to the dock. She's terrified of the Island and for good reason. Belle isn't the only bloodthirsty monster within our woods.

"To talk to the devil herself."

***

I hear the clink of heels echoing off the stone walls before I see her. Belle is beautiful, dressed in a glittering dress spun from the silk of butterfly wings, but all the Fae are a gift to the eyes. Or so I've been told.

Today, her long blonde hair is pulled into a bun at the top of her head, tied with a vine of green leaves and delicate yellow flowers. Tonight's gown reveals the scars of her past. She wears them with pride, unbothered by the two long marks that run from the center of each shoulder blade to the middle of her exposed back.

The skin there is a tender shade of pink and raw, the edges

around her scars bruised purple as if her wings had just been ripped from her flesh. But she lost them ages ago in the war against her people. Her father, the late King, ripped them off of her himself, robbing her of ancestral magic.

It's why Belle needs the memories of the dead. She draws on forbidden blood magic to keep herself in power, but the balance only lasts as long as Neverland's current king reigns.

Peter.

"You're late." Belle sneers, striding past me without sparing a passing glance, heading toward her chambers.

I follow, obedient as always. Forever playing my part to keep those I care about an arm's length from danger. "I'm sorry, my queen."

Belle pushes open the door to her room. Her fingers reach for the thin straps of her dress as she steps inside the door closes and I quickly lock it to make sure we won't be any interrupted. Per her usual orders. Even though her soldiers are mindless drones, and have never even thought to look in on what we do, no matter how loud she makes me scream.

Belle glances back, her brows furrowing with disdain. "Why are your clothes still on?"

"We have a problem," I confess.

"That we do," she purrs, running her fingernails down my chest. With practiced ease, she unbuttons my pants and wraps her hand around me. "Your cock isn't inside me yet."

This is the moment when I usually close my eyes and mentally transport myself somewhere else, with anyone but her.

A lifetime ago, I found Belle feasting on Harper, one of the few survivors from the original shipwreck. She tore into him, ravaging his body like a starved animal, then began hunting for the next soul to feast on. I panicked. It was my fault we were trapped on the Island. My fault the crew and my kids died. I didn't want any more blood on my hands. So I struck a deal with her, offering anything she wanted as long as she swore off killing my kind.

I didn't know what making a deal with the Fae would cost or how every word is twisted in their favor. I thought I offered her myself in place of the survivors. I thought she would feed on me and leave the rest alone.

I didn't specify how long she needed to stay away from the others, so in her mind, she didn't break her word. The last crew member died two days later. The only souls left were me, Peter, and Wendy. I refused to let her have them, so I found her someone else to feed on. The first Lost I ferried to the Island.

"There are no new souls in Neverland."

Belle stops rubbing my length and meets my gaze. "What do you mean there are no new souls?"

I find her stare and hold it. She sees my boldness as bravery when really, I just don't give a fuck anymore. "We've circled the Island and found no one."

Belle crosses the room and grabs a silk robe to cover herself with. "No one willing to stay?"

"No. I mean not a single soul in the waters. There isn't anyone to ferry into the next life."

"That's impossible." She chews on her thumbnail and paces the room. The skinny heels of her shoes and the beating of my heart in my ears are the only sounds until she finally asks, "How long?"

"A week."

"Why didn't you tell me this sooner?" she demands, her voice brimming with anger.

"I needed to be certain. I didn't want to raise any alarms if the gods hadn't changed the path to the afterlife to avoid the Island, but it seems they have."

"The gods aren't the problem. Neverland is. It's shifting." She pauses, contemplating what could be the cause. "Something has changed."

I tuck myself back into my pants, grateful not to have to perform tonight. I don't take pleasure in satisfying Belle. Her tastes are rougher than mine, although my skin seems to have hardened over the years. Her nails draw less blood each time she digs them into my back and I heal faster. The past few times, I've even made it to the cove and put my shirt on without ruining it.

"It's that girl." She sneers.

"Who?" I ask, hoping she doesn't know about Wednesday, but Belle knows everything. The Island whispers to her, just like it does to Peter.

Her glare turns sinister as she changes the topic. "You know the deal, James. I need to feed."

I nod and pull my shirt over my head, my body forever at her beck and call. That was the deal. This is what I thought she wanted all those years ago.

Belle positions herself behind me, her fingers gripping my shoulders. "Your memories are always the tastiest." She presses her lips to the side of my neck. "Anything you'd like to forget?"

"I don't care. Just do it," I reply, my tone heavy with resignation.

Belle sinks her teeth into my neck and a searing pain spreads through my body like poison in water. She swallows mouthful after mouthful of my blood, searching for a memory worth taking. For the others, they have no control. She latches onto the most precious parts of their past, the core memories that shaped them because those are the strongest. She rips that part of their life away even as the body fights to hold on. It's a painful tug of war that usually ends when the soul has collapsed at her feet, too weak to fight any longer.

It's then that I collect them and take them to the Inn, where the lost soul is nursed back to health, but they aren't the same. They sense the void, the absence of something vital, and the unknown gnaws at their consciousness.

But because I've sacrificed myself more than any other being on the Island. I know how to shield the important parts of myself. I give Belle a memory from my childhood. One that feels important but has no true meaning. I feel the moment it leaves me. Ice coats my insides, turning my blood cold. She sucks away the last Christmas I had before my mother passed. Thousands of wounds, cut by invisible knives, slice me to release the memory as another part of my soul dies, and then Belle releases me. She steps back, wipes her mouth with her thumb, and licks that finger.

"Such sweet sorrow." She hands me a towel to press against my wound. "I wish you would fight me, though. The memories are so much sweeter when the souls refuse to give up their past."

I hold the cloth to the bite mark. It will be healed in a few hours, but I'd rather not ruin my shirt while waiting for the hole to close. "I gave up fighting yeh decades ago. Why start now?"

"This won't last more than a few days, James. Your memories are the sweetest because I uncover another layer under your thick skin, but they don't satisfy me the way fresh meat does. I'll need more blood. Soon."

"I understand."

"We have a whole island of souls. If you can't find me new ones, I expect you to bring a pirate to me next time."

"Understood." I grab my shirt off the floor and turn to leave, but Belle slows my movements. She's strongest after a feed, not needing her dust to sway the hand of time.

"Where do you think you're going?" She tisks. "I haven't had my way with you yet."

CHAPTER 6
James

My shirt clings to my back, drenched and saturated with blood. I abandoned any hope of salvaging it nearly an hour ago when the bloodsuckers emerged from their hiding places within the Neverwoods. The mutated mosquitoes swarmed me the moment I ventured out of Belle's mountainside castle. They still hover, occasionally attempting to latch onto my skin, but their teeth can't break the cotton fabric.

I lean against the wall and hide in the shadows of Shelly's Seafood Shack. I should have regained my strength or, at the very least, stopped bleeding by now. I reach up and touch the bite mark and there's a squishing sound when my fingers meet the raw skin. Dark spots float in my vision. I should eat something, maybe even rest, but not here.

I whistle once, knowing Smee is somewhere on the deck, watching, waiting for my return. She hates coming into the Cove and does everything she can not to step foot on our grounds, but that whistle is our safe word. Spelled long ago to travel any lengths. It's not something either of us uses lightly. I close my eyes, too tired to keep them open and wait.

"Stars in the sky." Smee touches my cheek, waking me from a slumber I didn't realize I'd fallen into. "What did she do to you?"

"Nothing I can't handle," I say as confidently as I can muster, but even I don't believe my words. I'm weak. Belle took more than I realized, possibly even more than she intended.

Smee grabs me by the arms and pulls me upright. I must have slid down the wall when I passed out because I don't remember shifting off my feet. The shooting pain in my back feels like a blade reopening the wounds, and I clench my teeth to keep from cursing and release the tension with a grunt.

"Bullshit." Smee ducks under my arm and attempts to support my weight. "I've never so much as seen you come back with a scratch."

"And I've never seen yeh set foot on the mainland."

She rolls her eyes and ignores how big of a deal her being here for me is. "What happened?"

"I don't want anyone to see me," I mutter. I am the leader of these lands—the embodiment of strength in the eyes of the pirates. If I'm viewed as weak or unable to care for our crew, the Cove could turn to chaos. Not because they would overthrow my reign but because the Island could.

"I'll deal with anyone who tries to cause problems," Smee says.

We make good time to the boat. If anyone caught sight of us, they remained hidden in the shadows and, for now, kept their mouths shut. We limp our way to my quarters on the ship, each step more arduous than the last.

I'm tired.

So, unnaturally, tired. All I want to do is close my eyes and...

"Hey!" Smee taps my cheeks. "You can't sleep, Cap. Not yet." She hurries to the other side of the room, pours me a glass of scotch, and grabs a wooden peg. "Drink this and then bite down."

I swallow the alcohol in one gulp. It burns, but that's a fire I enjoy. I take the peg before the Scotch and fear can settle in my stomach and put it between my teeth. Smee tears my shirt at the collar until the fabric hangs off my shoulder. She sucks in a breath, taking in the claw marks and bite wound. There's only been a handful of times where I've needed her help after a visit with Belle. Based on her silence, I sense this might be the messiest aftermath to date.

"This is gonna hurt."

"Just do it," I grit.

Smee threads a needle and then pokes the end through my severed skin. I bite down hard on the peg and grip the side of the couch. This hurts more than when Belle stuck her teeth in me. Smee threads in and out, pulling the hole shut as she goes.

"Almost done," she says, leaving out the second half of her sentence. *With this one.*

Eight stitches and my shoulder is mended. Another twelve in various places along my spine and my back has finally ceased to bleed.

"This isn't right," Smee says as she helps me into a clean shirt once I'm bandaged. "I've never seen anyone bleed this much. Not in Neverland."

"The Island is changing." My hands shake as I pour myself another glass of scotch. I should probably go down to the Galley and eat, but numbing the pain seems more appealing.

"Is that possible?"

"It's Neverland," I say halfheartedly. I swallow the liquid; its burn is a dull warmth compared to the searing pain from my stitches. "Anything is possible."

Smee chews on her bottom lip and loses herself in her thoughts. She's only been with me for the last decade or so, but that's longer than all the rest. There's so much to this island I wish I could show her, but the stronger Belle gets, the more dangerous it is to venture outside of our cove.

"Could explain why the tides have changed."

"What did yeh say?" I ask, unsure if I heard her right whilst setting my glass on the counter.

Smee hitches her thumb over her shoulder and looks at me, puzzled. "The tide. It's going out."

Adrenaline has me pushing through the pain and hobbling out to the deck to look over the rail. Far-off waves push the water onto our shoreline, but with each new rush, the water doesn't touch the sand where it last kissed.

Smee is right. The tide has shifted for the first time since I set foot in Neverland.

"Smee," I say excitedly. "Ready the sails."

"Where are we going?" She follows me, probably convinced I'm crazy, yet she still rings the bell to signal the crew. They'll all be here soon, ready to take the old girl out to sea again.

I hurry back to my quarters and pull out my maps. I've drawn every inch of the Island and the waters surrounding it. I've sailed to the horizon, only to be cast out to the other side of my map, but today will be different. I can feel it in my bones.

"James?" she asks cautiously. "There aren't any souls in the water. We already looked today."

"We aren't looking for souls." I roll the papers and tuck them under my arm. Time is ticking away. Each second is precious and every one lost could mean the difference between making it there or not. I look at my crew, eight sailors who have sworn themselves to me. I smile, proud of the men and women I've come to call my friends, then meet Smee's gaze. "We're going to fetch ourselves a Darling."

I've watched and waited for Heidi to show signs of life, but there's nothing. We've had injuries in Neverland before, bad ones that would have killed the soul if it were anywhere else. The worst was when Scarlett almost beheaded Emmit last summer, but even his wounds healed. In a matter of minutes, he was back to his old self, laughing and calling himself Nearly Headless Em.

There was never any doubt that he'd be okay because the wound stopped bleeding and the skin stitched itself back together almost as soon as the blade passed through. The longest we've ever waited for someone to heal was five minutes, and that was stressful. But this, watching the life fade from someone both Peter and I care about, is excruciating.

"She's not healing? Why isn't she healing?" I plead, my voice quivering with fear.

This was Emmit's island before it became ours. He should know its rules better than any of us. I want him to tell me that Belle's dust is delaying the healing process and that once it wears off, Heidi will be fine. She'll wake up pissed with a minor headache, but she'll be okay.

But the longer it takes him to answer me, the less likely that feels.

Emmit's gaze remains fixed on Heidi's body lifelessly sprawled on the cold dungeon floor, surrounded by a pool of her blood. His silence feels like a weight pushing a truth I don't want to swallow down my throat.

I've witnessed horrible things as Neverland's Shadow, but I've never seen anyone die.

"Belle was wrong, you know," Emmit mutters. "I wouldn't have been able to save her. That's not how my gift works."

There are only three fairies left on the Island—Belle, Cass, and Emmit. Cass was never shy about his powers. He was happy to add touches of Forever Frost all around our little compound to make things more comfortable for the Lost.

I learned about Belle's ability to manipulate time while I was in shadow form, witnessing the extent of her cruelty firsthand as she used her dust to drag out the suffering of her victims. But Emmit has never used or even hinted at his gifts.

Peter never asked what he could do, and up until now, I've never been able to. "Why would she say it then? What can you do?"

Emmit shakes his head, his gaze falling to the ground. "It doesn't matter."

A heavy silence hangs between us, pregnant with questions I sense he doesn't want to answer, but I am not Peter. I won't push my curiosities aside for the sake of making others comfortable. If Emmit can do something to save The Lost or if he can help us out of this mess, I need to know what that is.

"How long will her dust last?" I ask, trying to steady my voice to sound like Peter's, but it shakes. The Island is changing. It's not listening to me anymore, and it's hurting the souls it used to protect.

I'm scared of what else it might do to them. Better yet, to me.

"Depends on how strong she is. This time freeze could last a few hours or a few days."

Days.

The notion brings a mix of relief and fear. Days would grant me time to strategize and plan to escape, but it would also keep me separated from Wednesday for longer than planned. I initially thought I would only be gone for a few weeks in her time, but now it seems like it might stretch to months. Stars above, I hope it's not years. However long it takes, she will despise me, thinking I abandoned her, but at least she'll be safe.

"You're not Peter," Emmit says, his voice barely a whisper. It's a statement, not a question.

I consider lying, but the gravity of our situation demands honesty. "Was I that obvious?"

"No, Belle would have devoured you if she knew." Emmit presses, urgency lacing his words. "Where is he?"

"I don't know," I admit, and that singular truth scares me more than any other I have to offer.

"What do you mean, you don't know? What happened out there?"

"Peter was dying. The mortal realm was reclaiming his spirit and he was too scared to leave Wednesday. He passed out in the hospital and I took over to give him a chance to rest. I thought crossing into Neverland would put him back in charge and kicked me out of his body. That's what usually happens, but he never came back. I can't even hear him."

"This isn't good."

"I know."

Emmit shakes his head. "I don't think you do. You were the one in command when you crossed into Neverland. Right?"

"Yeah. So?"

"There can only be one reigning king and you're not him," Emmit emphasizes, his words hitting me like a sudden blow. He clenches his hands again, tugging at the chains relentlessly.

"Emmit! What is going on?" I whisper yell. I don't know if Belle has guards that would tell her what they overhear or if the room is spelled to carry our voices across her castle. I shouldn't risk anyone listening to our conversation, but I need answers.

"By the laws of our land, you killed the king, which means the Island will choose a new ruler. Everything we know about Neverland is about to change," Emmit explains.

"I didn't kill him. I'm right here."

"Exactly. You," Emmit points out, his finger jabbing toward me. "Not Peter."

CHAPTER 8
Wednesday

I let out a piercing scream, the pain ripping through me, unbearable and relentless. A small part of me wishes I listened to Tyle and went to the hospital to deliver, but I couldn't risk it. My pregnancy may have been normal, easy even compared to what I expected, but there's still a chance this baby could be born different.

"I can see the head!" Tyle says excitedly. "One more push, Wednesday. You can do this."

I shake my head, tears mingling with sweat as another contraction seizes my body. The pain spreads from my lower back, down my legs, and wraps around my chest. I can't breathe, can't think beyond the building pressure.

"Push!" Tyle yells.

"Now!" Peter's voice echoes in my ear. He's been a constant throughout my pregnancy, a whisper in my mind, an intangible presence. A figment of longing my imagination conjured to ease the sting of being abandoned.

I scream once more, summoning every ounce of strength I have left, as pins and needles crawl up my spine, overwhelming every sensation until the pressure suddenly releases, leaving me breathless. I collapse onto the air mattress we blew up on the living room floor, an exhausted, sweaty mess.

"It's a girl," Tyle says, moving closer to my side.

I struggle to prop myself up on my trembling arms and gaze at the tiny bundle of blonde hair wrapped in a terry-cloth towel. She's beautiful.

She's blonde.

Oh, fuck. I sink back onto the air mattress and silent tears stream down my cheeks as I realize what that means.

"Hey," Tyle coos, attempting to console me. "It's ok. You don't have to see her. I have a friend in child services who could—"

"No!" I wipe my eyes and pull myself together. Today is a good day, a happy day.

I hold out my hands and Tyle carefully places the baby girl in my trembling arms. "I just needed a minute."

"Does she look like him?" My sister asks softly.

"Who?"

"Peter."

"No," I say solemnly, although I wish my baby girl did. "The baby isn't his."

Tyle's eyes widen with shock. "There were others? You had to—"

"No," I interject flatly. "I chose to be with Cass."

"So, you're relieved?" she asks, confused. I get it. Everything that happened in Neverland is confusing, and she barely knows half of it. "Those are happy tears?"

"Yeah, Tyle," I lie. "I'm happy."

"What are you going to call her?"

I hesitate. I toyed with so many names, but none of them felt right. Waverly. Willow. Wendeline. Now that I see her, I understand why they were wrong.

"Mira," I say confidently. That name was never on my radar, but it came to me the moment I laid eyes on her. "Because she's my little miracle."

***

I sit in my old room and watch Mira sleep. Tyle converted it into a playroom for the kids after I refused to move in. We both agreed that the three of us—her, Kenny, and me— under one roof would be a recipe for disaster.

Instead, we transformed the detached garage into a one-bedroom suite for me and Mira. I'm close enough to help with the kids but far enough away to have some privacy. It's worked out well, especially since Tyle went back to work in the office last month.

But I reluctantly agreed to sleep in my old room for the next few nights. Tyle insists I should be close in case I need an extra pair of hands, but I think she just misses the new baby smell. Wanda is walking and talking, ready to conquer the world, while Wyatt is crawling, eager to chase after her.

I place my hand on Mira's chest, a surge of terror coursing through me along with the irrational fear she'll stop breathing. Her heart beats steadily beneath my touch as my hand rises and falls in rhythm with her breaths. I stare at her in awe, still struggling to believe that I brought such a beautiful thing into this world. Despite partly belonging to Cass, she's perfect.

"You should eat," my sister's voice drifts from the doorway.

"I don't want to leave her," I say without looking away.

"I get it; being a new mom is scary." Tyle takes me by the hand and pulls me out of the rocking chair. "But you've got to take care of yourself, too, Mama. Mira isn't going anywhere. The kitchen is just downstairs and you can watch her on the video monitor while you're there."

I don't want to leave. Something in me aches at the thought of walking away, even just for a few minutes, but Tyle is right. Mira is settled. Safe. And I am hungry.

I follow Tyle downstairs. As soon as we're in the kitchen she pulls out all the fixings to make me a sandwich. She goes through Mom's motions, cutting off the edges and sectioning it into quarters. Just like she does for her kids. Something I plan to do for my own daughter.

How crazy is that? I have a child.

"What made you decide against the traditional W?" Tyle asks, pulling me from the comfort of my thoughts.

"An M is an upside-down W. I figured it was close enough."

Tyle laughs, then picks the sugary bits off of the blueberry muffin she bought for breakfast this morning. "And here I thought I would be the rebellious one."

A sudden chill sends a shiver down my spine. I wait for the familiar whisper that usually accompanies the sensation, but my mind remains eerily silent.

"You okay?" Tyle asks, concern etched on her face.

"Yeah, I've just got a weird feeling," I say as a sense of unease settles over me. "I'm going to check on Mira."

"Wens, she's fine," Tyle reassures me, adjusting the monitor to face me. "See?"

"*Hurry!*" Peter's voice shouts in my ears.

I jump off the barstool, startled to have heard him so clearly, and sprint up the stairs. My heart pounds in my chest as Peter continues to yell, *"Faster, Darling! Run!"*

I skid to a stop in the doorway as a figure bends over Mira's bassinet. I know him, even without seeing his face. That Jack Frost blonde hair. The chill that follows wherever he goes. The heart-racing excitement drenched in fear.

"You did well, Darling." Cass turns toward me, cradling Mira in his arms. "She's beautiful."

"Give me back my daughter," I seethe.

"Our daughter," he corrects, a hint of menace in his voice.

"Cass," I warn, my voice trembling. I never thought I'd see him again. I didn't even know he could leave the Island. But I try to be strong for Mira. Scared or not, I'll do anything to keep her safe. "I swear to the stars, I'll kill you if you don't hand her over."

"Your threats are useless, whereas mine..." He pauses, barely looking at me, and ice spreads like spider webs across the floor.

"What do you want?"

"Nothing you can give me, but her..." Cass looks down at my daughter and their resemblance is uncanny. "She can give me the world."

"Cass." I step forward, determination burning in my eyes. I

don't know what he has planned but, knowing him, it can't be good.

"Say goodbye to Mommy, Mira."

"Cass!" I lunge at him, but instead of colliding with a body, I pass through a burst of snow and crash into the bassinet.

I push through the swirling flakes, scattering them across the floor, searching for a portal or a marker of some sort—anything that can lead me back to Neverland.

"Wens?" Tyle's voice fills the room. She freezes in the doorway, her eyes widening as she takes in the ice and snow invading her home in the middle of May. "What's happening?"

"He took her!" I say frantically. Tears fill my eyes as I realize that I can't follow them to Neverland. I'm stranded in this world, alone again, while my daughter is with a monster.

"Who?"

"Cass."

"The man you said was her father?" Tyle tries to put the pieces together, but she doesn't have enough clues to make everything line up. I left so much out of my story, too many details about where I was and with whom.

I don't have the strength to explain. I'm physically exhausted from giving birth, in pain from my fall, and emotionally in shock. I nod because right now, that's all I can do.

"Where'd they go?"

"To Neverland."

"You can't be serious," Tyle says in disbelief. "Is that what they called the place they took you to? That's so fucked up."

She starts rattling on about trauma and triggers, and I vaguely hear her mention something about calling the cops, but I'm only half listening.

Pan said he and Peter argued for hours about how to bring me to Neverland, which means it's possible to get there without dying. I decide right then that I don't care what I have to do or how long it takes; I'm going to get my daughter back.

CHAPTER 9
Wednesday

"Thank you, officers. We'll be in touch." Kenny closes the front door and rejoins Tyle and me in the living room. She's holding Wyatt close, rocking him to keep him quiet. Silently basking in relief that he wasn't the child stolen.

I hold a cup of tea in my hands. It's gone cold waiting for me to take a sip. I don't like it cold. The cold brings me back to the nursery and to the frost that has yet to melt on the wooden floors. The cops called it a scientific bio-weapon. They said I was lucky it didn't touch me. They couldn't be more right and wrong if I spelled it out for them.

"Your description was really helpful," Tyle says, trying to reassure me, but nothing she says will ease the ache in my chest. "I bet they'll have a sketch drawn up lickety-split. Cass's face will be all over the news by sundown."

It won't make a difference. The cops could post Cass's face on every billboard across the globe and no one would find him.

"Wens?" Kenny gingerly touches my arm. I jump in my seat, startled by how cold his hand is, and spill the tea all over their couch cushion and my leg.

"Sorry," I say, frantically searching for a napkin to soak up the liquid before it stains the upholstery.

Kenny drops to his knees before me and takes my hand. He sets my cup on the coffee table beside us and looks me in the eyes. "It's going to be okay."

I force a tight-lipped smile and nod. "I know."

"It's nearly dark," Tyle says. "Is anyone hungry?"

I look out the window. She's right. It's twilight. The only

time when the veil between my world and theirs is thin enough to pass through.

I push Kenny aside and run upstairs to my old room. It's the same disheveled mess, only worse now that the cops have trampled through and I drop to the ground and touch the ice trails. They've etched themselves into the wood like burn marks. I crawl on my hands and knees, searching for anything that might be different. Waiting for Peter to speak up and guide me home, but he's been eerily quiet since Mira left. I can't even feel his presence anymore.

"Wednesday?" Tyle asks cautiously. "What are you doing?"

"Looking?"

"For what?" she asks, probably thinking I've lost my mind.

I sit back on my legs, frustrated. "I don't know, a clue. Something that could tell me where he's gone or might go. Anything, really."

"Sweetie, there's nothing here."

"I know," I say reluctantly.

"And there's nothing you can do right now," she adds.

I know that, too, but I don't want to admit it because saying that out loud feels like giving up.

"Unless you can tell the police more details about the Island you lived on or something about Cass's past that could help track him down, you just need to sit tight."

"I don't know anything about his past, but I do know a little about Peter's," I say, an idea forming. "Tyle, I need your passport."

"What?" She looks at me, startled, then shakes her head. "No! Why?"

"Peter mentioned having family in London. I could go there and find them."

"Do you realize how crazy that sounds?"

"Yes, but I have to try, Tyle. It's the only lead I have." England is where the Peter Pan stories originated. There's bound to be something tangible I can grab onto there. Wendy's original journals. A paper trail of Peter's estate and what happened to it. Or maybe I can find the bank holding all of Peter's money and find out how he's been contacting them. I might not have a solid plan yet, but I know I'll learn something there. I just know it.

"No."

"Tyle!" I shout, frustrated and on the brink of tears.

"No! I'm not going to support you running away to chase after that man. Peter's not the one who stole your baby. He can't help you."

"You don't know that!"

"Neither do you!"

"I'm going," I say, my voice firm. "Either you give me your passport, or I'll find someone to forge me one."

"Here." Kenny steps into the room, holding a little blue booklet.

"Kenny!" Tyle yells. "What the hell?"

"You can't mamma-bear her, Tyle. It won't work. Either support Wednesday and have a relationship when she comes back, or fight her tooth and nail and lose her forever."

"I don't want you to leave." She takes the passport from her husband and hands it to me.

"I know, but I have to go." I pull her in for a hug. This feels like the beginning of goodbye and I'm surprised at how much I don't want to go. Tyle became an unexpected anchor in my life, but I can't stay. "You'd cross oceans for Wanda and Wyatt, wouldn't you?"

"In a heartbeat," she says without hesitation.

"Well, that's what I'm going to do. I don't care how long it takes; I'm finding my daughter."

"Okay. Just promise me you won't disappear again. I can't lose you twice."

I force another smile. My heart breaks because if I find a way to Neverland, I can't guarantee I'll be able to come back. But Tyle doesn't need to suffer through that pain just yet. I'll call her every day and reassure her of how grateful I am for her these past few months. I'll make sure she knows she's loved and that, no matter what, I'll never forget her. I agree to her promise because today I can keep it.

Tomorrow...

I make no promises about what the future holds.

CHAPTER 10

A large wave crashes over the bow of the Jolly Roger. The Neversea is angry, trying to hold us back, but we've come further than we ever have before. I hold the helm with both hands while the winds and waves try to force me to return to the Island.

Smee hangs onto the railing as she climbs the steps to meet me on the quarterdeck. Another wave washes over the side, drenching her, nearly dragging her to the trenches of the Neversea, but she hangs tight. The boat rocks to the other side, affording her a brief moment to reach me before it tips the other way, and we're soaked again.

"Yeh should be below deck," I tell her. Sea water drops off my hair and into my eyes. I wipe it away quickly, only able to fight the ocean with one hand for so long. "It isn't safe up here."

"I don't think she can take much more of this," Smee says, ignoring my request.

"She's a good ship. She'll be fine." I hope.

I built the Jolly Roger from scraps of Mariner, the first ship I sailed to Neverland. Pieces of her floated to shore, as well as remnants of other boats the Neversea claimed. It took a few years and a lot of trial and error, but she's held strong since her maiden voyage.

I wince as seawater washes over the deck, this time from behind. The salty spray clings to my shirt, probably staining it red as it saturates my bandages.

Belle's marks are closed thanks to Smee's quick work with a needle, but the skin is still sore. My cuts haven't healed like they ought to have, and the bite mark on my neck is festering. The dark purple veins around the wound and her poison has spread in the last three days from a tight-knit circle into tendrils reaching down my back and over my shoulder. I can't worry about what will happen if they reach my heart. Right now, the goal is to make it out of this storm alive. And then find Wednesday.

"Cap?" Smee asks wearily. She points to a dark mass in the water. "What is that?"

"The gates of hell," I say, half-teasing, but it's precisely what I'm looking for. I spin the wheel, banking us hard to the left and straight toward the mouth of the beast.

The ocean fights to keep us away from the portal to the realm of the living. She throws us from side to side, begging us to turn around, but we can't go back. Not until we have the Darling.

Smee loses her footing and slides across the deck. My heart lurches because I can't help her. We'll lose control of the ship if I do. I watch, terrified that my first mate will go over, but she grabs onto the taffrail just in time.

"Get below deck," I order once Smee is on her feet again.

That was too close a call. Our code dictates we care for the crew over the sailor. If someone falls over, they're gone. Plus, once a soul is pulled from the Neversea, it can't go back. The deep waters will eat through them like acid. There are minutes, if that, to save them, but if rescuing one means damning the rest...

Well, everyone here knows the risk of coming aboard.

"No," Smee states firmly.

"That wasn't a request."

"I'm not going anywhere, James."

"Stubborn ass woman!" I fire off, half-teasing. She is stubborn, but I wouldn't have her any other way.

"Ungrateful scallywag!" she spits back, grinning. "What's the plan?"

"We're going to sail into the whirlpool and hope to come out the other side."

Smee looks to the darkened water, thrashing with whitecaps, then back to me. My plan is as, if not more, reckless as it sounds. "Seriously?"

"If yeh've got a better way to cross between realms, I'm all ears."

"Fucking hell." Smee grabs a nearby dock rope and wraps it around her waist. "If we die, I'm finding your ass in the next life and killing you."

"Duly noted. Now hang on!"

The ship groans as we slide into the vortex. Something cracks and lightning thunders from above. Dark clouds in a once-blue sky begin to rain down on us, sending another warning that I stupidly ignored the first time I crossed into these waters. This time, I know what it means. Sink or swim, ride or die, our world is about to change.

"Get ready to hold yehr breath!" I yell over the sound of lightning and rushing water. I don't know if Smee hears me, but I take in a big gulp of air just as the ship falls into the center of the whirlpool and we're surrounded by water.

CHAPTER 11

Scarlett's screams echo in the damp dungeon. She's the first to wake from Belle's time spell. I have a feeling Belle let her dust wear off so I can see my friend's suffering before being forced to watch another die.

I still have hope the Island will heal Heidi's wounds, but that hope is fleeting. Her skin lost its golden hue, possibly two days ago. That guess comes from the timeline of when Emmit and I got our last meal. If you could call crackers and a slice of ham a meal, but it's better than fully starving. Belle has fed and watered us just enough to keep our bodies from shutting down so she can drag out our pain.

"Scar," Emmit says in a tone meant to calm her. "Look at me, not Heidi."

Scarlett's cries turn frantic. She sags against the wall, her arms stretching tight as she turns into a useless bundle of emotions. Emmit tries his best to soothe her, but the girl needs a hug—something neither of us can provide.

"Scarlett!" I say, my voice booming through the room.

She looks at me, eyes wide because Peter never yells, but her cries have temporarily ceased. I've shocked her enough to derail her train of thought. It's time to put her to use and make a break for it.

Emmit's face pinches together as his head moves from side to side in a warning. A tinkling sound rings in my ears. A language I haven't heard in ages but recognize—the voice of the Fae.

Act like Peter, he cautions. *Not his shadow.*

"We don't have long before the others wake or Belle comes

back," I warn, trying my hardest not to scare her. Scarlett is like a baby deer, curious but skittish. One wrong move and the thread she's holding onto will snap.

"Belle?" Scarlett asks, her eyes widening with the realization that we aren't playing a game. Peter liked to play games, never this dark or cruel, but the Lost partook in some twisted games nonetheless.

"I need you to pull yourself together," I say slowly. "Your chains, can you get your hands out of them?"

"What?"

"Goddamn it, woman, your wrists!" I take a breath and summon every bit of strength I have left not to shout. I let the air out slowly, then use my most placating voice to say, "You're so tiny. Do you think you can slip out of the chains?"

Scarlett twists and tugs against her bindings. Her arms move, but not enough. The metal cuffs are smaller than her knuckles. They won't slip past. "I can't."

"What if you break your thumbs? Maybe if you dislocate the bones, your hand will be small enough to slip free." Logic to save our lives. But fear and pain can alter the brain, and Scarlett is in shock, not survival mode.

"What! No!" Scar shakes her head. "What's gotten into you?"

"It's not a bad idea," Emmit mumbles. "I can't heal him," he adds, meeting Scarlett's gaze. "But I can heal you. It'll only hurt for a few minutes."

"Have you two lost your minds?"

"There's a reason you're awake and the others aren't," I lie, but half suspect the admission to be true. Every move Belle makes is calculated. We are pawns in her game and she'll wipe us off the board if we're not smart and careful. "When Belle realizes you're no longer asleep, she'll come for you next."

Scarlett looks from me to Emmit. Her eyes are wide and wet with new tears. "You think she'll kill me?"

I swear to the stars and gods and Fae and every other deity out there, if this woman asks me another pointless question, I might just kill her myself. "Yes, Scar. Belle's a little mad and using all of you as leverage to try and force me to tell her where Wednesday is."

"So, tell her!" Scarlett squeals.

"She'll still kill us," Emmit adds, bringing home my point. "Just because she can. You escaping and setting us free is our best chance at surviving right now. Not what you want to hear, but it's true."

A new sob leaves Scarlett's lips. She wastes precious minutes working through her emotions, and we have no choice except to wait and hope Belle doesn't walk in to make her next kill.

Scarlett sniffles and looks at Emmit. Her face is red and blotchy, her eyes glassy pools of grief. Her breaths come in shallow gasps, but her words are steady. "You're sure you can fix me?"

Emmit nods. "The first hand is going to be the most painful. Try not to scream. The second should go faster because you can snap the bones out of place. Once you're free, come straight to me."

"Okay," Scarlett whispers.

For the first time since I left Wednesday, I have a shred of hope we might escape. Not the panicked kind that clung to Heidi, but a pure wishful chance. But hope is a tricky devil. It skews one's perspective, diverting focus from reality to an improbability.

Scarlet tugs and tries her best to slip free. Her skin pulls as it drags against the metal bindings. She bites her lip to keep from crying out, but her wrist isn't moving, not the way it should. She can't manipulate the bones enough on her own.

I reach for my powers, even though they haven't listened to me since I arrived, and beg for the Island to free her by any means possible. I wait and hope for the sensation of the Never-land's magic to fill me, but I'm hollow inside. Void of the only feeling I've truly ever known.

Peter has disappeared and the Island has abandoned me.

Despite being surrounded by friends, I am alone for the first time in my life.

"It's okay," I tell her as the reality that this is where our lives ends sinks in. "You did your best."

Scarlett nods her head, unable to speak. I'm sure she's in pain, and the realization that Belle will be coming for her soon is probably hitting home.

I drop my head and close my eyes. I'm tired. This body is fading, even with the food Belle feeds us. I'm not sure how much longer it will last.

I think of Wednesday and smile at how big she must be. I wonder if she's had the child yet and if it's a boy or a girl. I bet she hates me for leaving without saying a word about its existence. If I had, I wouldn't have been able to leave her behind. I needed to pretend the baby wasn't there and hope to be back in time for either Peter or me to be by her side for it's birth.

But I've failed her.

And the little one.

"Ow," Scarlett mumbles and there's a new clanking sound. I open my eyes, and she's rubbing her hip with her hand.

I stare at the fallen shackles in disbelief. The Island listened. Please tell me it heard me and actually listened! "How did you get free?"

"I don't know. They just popped open. What now?"

I'm so excited I could fly, but my happy thoughts aren't enough to lift me off my feet. Still, I have hope again. Neverland may have stripped me bare of my magic, but she hasn't left me to die.

"They're simple locks," Emmit directs. "A twist and latch, but no key is needed. They're meant for the Fae, not mortal souls."

Scarlett goes to him first and just as he said, all she needs to do is twist a small knob and flip the latch for him to be set free.

Emmit's wrists look terrible, red and blistered from the metal burns, but he takes Scarlett's hands in his and starts muttering under his breath.

"Thank you," she says when he lets her go.

Emmit nods, but he looks weaker, aged at least another two or three years, too. "Help Peter, then release the others. I'll find us a way out of here."

Scarlett hurriedly unlatches my bindings. My arms ache, finally released from the awkward position, but it's a good ache. I grab Emmit by the elbow as he passes. He stops and looks at me, but the spark in his eyes is fading.

"Are you okay?" I ask.

"Nothing comes free." He holds up his hand and there are new marks on his wrist. "When I heal someone, I take on their injuries. To save Heidi would have meant killing myself. I loved her, but her life wasn't worth sacrificing mine for."

I nod, understanding, and let him go. The only person in all the worlds I'd die for is the Darling, and that's only if it were a last resort.

It takes a few feeble minutes to free Xyris and Aria from their shackles. I help lower them to the floor. Belle's dust hasn't worn off yet, but I have a feeling it will soon.

Aria's skin is in worse shape than Emmit's. Burn marks cover her arms and back. The charred black skin is angry, and her wrists have rubbed themselves nearly to the bone. She's going to be in a lot of pain when she wakes up.

"I found a way out," Emmit says, coming back into the room. "But we don't have a lot of time."

He picks Xyris up, cradling him in his arms while I reach for Aria. I'm careful with how I hold her. Even the slightest touch pulls away the paper-thin skin around her burns.

"What about Heidi?" Scarlett asks. Her gaze bounces from Emmit to me as we have a silent conversation.

"I can't carry both of them and keep Aria's skin intact, and you're too weak," I say to Emmit, the language of the Fae coming back to me. I'm not sure if I'm getting everything right, but he seems to follow what I'm trying to say.

I could try...

Don't, Emmit. You need to save your strength. Peter would understand if we have to sacrifice one to save the group.

He chuckles lightly but I don't think Scarlett hears it. *You sound like a pirate.*

That's possibly the worst insult I've ever been given. They're loyaless souls, blindly following a *Captain* who knowingly feeds their memories to Belle to save his own skin. James is spineless and has zero regard for the hell he's put Neverland through.

As much as I hate the man, I try to sound like James when I tell Scarlett, "Heidi is literally dead weight. We have to leave her."

Scarlett's mouth falls open. Abandoning one of his own is something Peter would never say. He'd find a way to save everyone, even if it meant sacrificing himself. "We can't! I won't."

"You're not strong enough to carry her and we can't." I lift Aria slightly in case Scarlett needs the reminder that my hands are already full. Her living friend needs me. Her dead one is already gone.

"If it helps, Heidi didn't feel anything when she died," Emmit adds. "We'll do a remembrance for her when it's safe, but you need to make a choice, Scar. Stay behind and die, too, or let her go and live."

Scarlett bites her bottom lip. Tears well in her eyes again, and I get it; it's hard to say goodbye. "This feels wrong."

"I know," I agree, "but staying here won't bring Heidi back. All it does is put you in danger and she wouldn't want that."

Scarlett sniffles and tries to hold in her tears. She's breaking, we all are, but doing her best to stay strong. "Is it wrong that I want to make Belle pay for what she did? Does that make me a bad person?"

"I'm not the right person to ask," I admit. If I could access my magic, I'd have struck Belle dead with a lightning bolt the moment she touched one of the Lost. The Island delivered them to Peter to keep their memories safe from Belle. I don't know why, but I'm sure it had its reasons. They were to be protected at all costs, and I lost one.

The weight of my failure feels like a knife in my lungs.

Maybe the Island took my magic as punishment. I left Neverland when it needed me most. Because of me, the Lost were unprotected.

"Why not?" she asks, but I don't answer.

Emmit saves me from answering and leads us down a dark corridor. There are no lights to guide us. The deeper we go, we can't see what's coming or what's been left behind. There's only the sound of our breaths and the pitter-patter of our steps.

Scarlett's question plays on a loop in my mind. Is it wrong to want payback for Heidi's death? No, I don't think it is. Why?

Because I intend to kill the bitch, and her brother, too.

Chapter 12
Wednesday

I see her sometimes, late at night when the stars fade into day and the alcohol is deep in my veins. Mira's beautiful face, with her thin blonde hair, peacefully sleeping in a wood-carved cradle. It's not often, only around the full moon when the veil between her world and mine is thin, but I look forward to the visions. Those nights, as hard as they may be, are better than the ones where I have nothing but my thoughts and dreamless sleep.

I poke at the ice cubes in my drink with a straw and wonder if she'll look any different tonight. I can always find something, a subtle change that marks her growth. A child's infancy is precious. Babies change so quickly that it's hard to appreciate the tiny milestones, like turning their heads. She's done that twice now, which tells me my original concept of Neverland time wasn't too far off.

My baby girl is approximately three weeks old.

Three Neverland weeks, the equivalent of nearly three years in this stupid world.

I'd give anything to be with Mira and have tried everything shy of killing myself to find her. My biggest hesitation is that doing so might not take me to her. I can't risk Cass being the only parent she knows. I am a firm believer that circumstance greatly influences a child. If all Mira knows are lies and deceit, she doesn't stand a chance at becoming the good-hearted person I know she's meant to be.

If I knew dying would take me to her, I'd do it in a heartbeat, but until I have guaranteed passage into Neverland, I'm not ready going that route.

I sip on my soda and wait for the night to slip away. There's no point in drinking just yet. I have to find that happy line between wasted and functional, or else I'll fall asleep and miss my chance to see her. I only get three nights a month.

Three precious nights I refuse to waste.

Tyle thinks I've lost my mind and maybe she's right. Maybe I dream of Mira because I can't let her go. And maybe the few times I've thought I've heard Peter's voice since she left were nothing but a symptom of insanity. If it is, I'm not ready to give up my craziness.

"Can I buy you a drink?" a deep voice asks.

I smile against my straw and glance at the man who's made himself comfortable to my right. He's handsome, with dark skin as smooth as chocolate and amber eyes. His wide smile is welcoming, but I know what he wants.

The answer I've yet to decide is, do I want it too? Will he be the one to finally fill the void Peter Pan left or will he be just another body to pass the time?

"Sure. I'll take a Scotch and soda," I say to the bartender.

"A woman with refined taste. I'm intrigued."

"Are you now?" I push my virgin drink aside and thank the bartender as he slides the mixed drink in front of me. The first sip is bitter. The bartender used the cheap shit, but I don't mind. It hits hard and fast. Exactly what I need if I'm going to make it through the night.

I tune my new friend out as he talks, not even catching this man's name, but I let him continue. I smile and nod when appropriate. I even manage to pitch into the conversation with small tidbits of nothing.

"I bet you would," I say when he mentions how he'd love to get to know me better.

I smile and talk and flirt until I've had enough drinks to where I feel sorry enough for myself to ask, "So, is this your plan? To sit here and buy me drinks all night, or will you ever make a move?"

"What did you have in mind?"

I toss back the last half of my cocktail—my fourth in less than an hour—and grab the man by the hand. I lead him to the back of the building where the bathrooms are.

It's almost midnight. I don't have time for hotel rooms and foreplay. I don't want to cuddle after the deed is done and fall asleep in his arms. I just want a good, hard fuck to feel halfway normal for five minutes.

"Move," I say to the lady at the front of the bathroom line.

"Fuck you! I have to pee!" she retorts. I don't blame her for being angry, but I've got a small window to feel good before my night takes me home. A few more drinks and a walk by the river after last call, and I'll finally get to see my baby girl.

Until then, I've got an emptiness inside me to try to fill and time to kill.

"Piss in a corner." I open my clutch, pull out a hundred-dollar bill, and shove it at her. "Then go buy yourself a new pair of panties."

I push forward as soon as the door opens, before the woman in line can skirt past, and lock both me and my new friend inside. I grab him by the waist of his pants as he says, "Fuck, that was hot."

I don't care to talk and make quick work with his belt to drop his pants. I fist his cock with my hand and pump his long, thick length. The guy drops his head and presses his lips to my neck while I mentally prepare myself to be stretched and stuffed. It's gonna hurt, but I welcome the pain. It reminds me that I'm alive and that I can feel something more than emptiness.

Mr. Big Dick slides his hand up my thigh to my center. He pushes my panties aside and dips one finger inside me. I wish I could say it feels good, but he's not who I want, so it just...feels.

"Don't tease me, baby," I pant, faking a breathless moan. "I want to feel you." Men like it when I tell them what I want, and this one caves at my whispers.

"You got it, sugar." He lifts me by the hips, onto the edge of the sink, and drives inside of me with one harsh push.

I wasn't ready. I cry out, the heat of accommodating someone so big almost too much to bear, and Mr. Big Dick takes it as a sign of endearment. He thrusts deeper. Harder.

I drop my head back against the mirror and stare at the drawn-on drop ceiling tiles. Eventually, this should start to feel good, but the dry friction and the sheer size of this man is a wickedly uncomfortable combination. Until it does, I fake breathless pants of pleasure.

"Seriously?" James's voice seeps into my thoughts. "Come now, Sunshine. Yeh can do better than this. Can't yeh?"

I almost smile at the familiarity. James sounds so real, so much like the man I met at the Cove. He's been a constant in Wendy's memories and she's pushed him into my dreams almost as much as she's pushed Peter. I never expected to miss a man I barely know, but I feel just as tied to her husband as I do Peter Pan. This living two lives, both mine and re-living hers, is confusing.

I roll my head to the side and gasp when I see pale blues encircled by a layer of charcoal looking at me. James's midnight black hair is longer, falling into his eyes, but when he smiles those same two dimples come out of hiding and warmth fills my belly. He's not dressed in a flowing white shirt or loose black pants like he was at Harper's Edge. He blends into this world, wearing dark skinny jeans and an ash-colored Henley.

I've never seen James outside of my dreams before. Not even in my reckless days, when I thought channeling Bella from *New Moon* would bring Peter's voice back after he left me. It's always been Mira, and occasionally, I get to sneak a glance at Cass when he's with her. Watching them in that twilight hour is like peering through a window.

They're so close, yet painfully far.

A tear slides down my cheek as I stare up at the ceiling tiles again. Maybe my sister is right. Maybe all of this is in my head and I *am* losing my shit.

The thrusting stops and Mr. Big Dick pulls out of me. I wait for him to tell me how he wants my body next, but in the span of a heartbeat there's a crashing sound. I open my eyes and find him lying unconscious on the dirty bathroom floor, his pants and boxers at his knees, the singular stall door still swinging and clanging against its lock.

James steps into my line of sight, blocking my view of Mr. Big Dick. He plants his hands on either side of the sink I'm perched on, boxing me in. He smells like cedar and the sea and the scent tugs at a memory. I'm not sure if it's mine or Wendy's but longing fills my chest. I reach for his cheek, half expecting my hand to go through his face like a mirage, but I touch skin. Warm, scruffy skin.

"This wasn't how I hoped to find yeh again, Sunshine." His frown is deep. I'd feel bad if he were truly here, embarrassed even, but he's not. My mind has either created an imaginary friend or blurred the face of someone who could look like James and is torturing me. "What are yeh doing?"

I shrug, still unconvinced I'm not having some weird drunken hallucination. "Trying to feel something."

"Right," he says as if he understands the gaping hole living has left.

The real James might. I've watched through Wendy's eyes as she drifted away from her marriage and pulled toward Peter. I felt her heartbreak as James fought for their relationship, even though he knew she was unfaithful. It's hard being able to relate to both sides of the story because both we're victims of circumstance. Neither one of us is destined for happiness.

"How's that working out for yeh?"

I shrug again. Clearly, it's not going so well. I'm having conversations with am imaginary man in public, my pseudo-date is passed out on the floor, and I haven't orgasmed in years.

Life is great.

James comes closer and brushes his nose along my jaw. My heart races as the warmth in my chest drifts lower. "I can make yeh feel again, Sunshine," he whispers, his breath hot against my ear. "All yeh have to do is ask."

Right. Just ask my imaginary ex-whatever to stick me with his non-existent dick because that's going to make me feel normal again. Wendy's memories filter into my conscious thoughts. For a moment, I'm her again—like I am in my dreams—tied to James's bed naked. He dips between our legs and the rush of pleasure she feels has me blushing.

Fingers trail along my jawline and pillow my bottom lip. The past fades away and for a heartbeat, I consider asking. What's the worst that can happen? I fall that much further down this rabbit hole of hell? I fuck yet another man in this dirty bathroom? Mr. Big Dick couldn't hit it right. Who knows, maybe this guy—if he's real—can. *Stars, I really am losing my mind.*

"Please."

"Say it, Sunshine." James's voice is a low growl that awakens something deep inside me. Anxiousness mixes with excitement and it has my resolve bending. "I've waited a long time to hear those words."

"Fuck me, James." Stars above, I hope this isn't some fucked up hallucination. If it is, though, I might have to buy stock in whatever kind of scotch that was. I'd drink it every night if I could.

James takes my chin between his thumb and forefinger and tilts my head. "As yeh wish."

CHAPTER 13

James

Finding the Darling was harder than I expected.

This world is bigger than I remembered. The streets are louder, the cities busier, and the magic it once held is damn near gone. Days passed, sailing along the coastlines, before I finally felt the same pull that sucked me into Harper's Edge weeks ago. The extraordinary thread that ties our past and the present together.

Peter thinks he and the Darling are soul mates, and that may be true, but she chose me in that life and the one before and was meant to in every life after had we not been sucked into Neverland. That's the beauty of rebirth. When a soul moves onto the next stage of their life, they find their way to their lovers once again.

So long as the Darling and I exist in the same realm I will always find her, love her, and then give her the choice of who she wants to be with.

However, discovering her in the dirty bathroom of a tavern being fucked by a man who has no business sticking his dick inside my Darling was not a part of the plan. But even the best-laid plans have hiccups.

"Fuck me, James," she whispers, her voice trembling.

A smirk tugs at my lips because I've waited too many years for my Darling to return. Her soul may love my brother, but this woman is unsure of what she wants. All she knows is that without us, she is incomplete.

But tonight, she'll learn what it means to feel whole again.

I pinch Wednesday's chin between my fingers and pull her

lips to mine. She holds back, probably unsure if this is what she truly desires. I give her time to decide, but I know what will happen. The moment she opens herself up to the idea of us, this world will find a spark of magic it lost long ago.

Wednesday's tongue pushes into my mouth and a jolt of energy courses through me. The air ripples around us in a way that would make me nervous if we were back on the Island but here the magic in the room has everything to do with us and nothing to do with Neverland.

Wednesday grabs me by the shirt and pulls me closer. She feels it too, this hum of life. I know she does. Her legs wrap around my waist and I lift her off the dirty counter. I don't need the help of the sink to support her. She's light as air in my arms.

Darling's fingers touch everything they can reach. My hair. Neck. Back. Her kisses are hungry, like she's been starved of life and I'll happily give her mine if that's what she needs.

Her nails brush over the stitches on my back and my muscles tighten as a ripple of pain fights the heat she emits. I ignore the discomfort and support Wednesday with one arm while my other hand finds my belt and I drop my pants.

"Are yeh sure about this, Sunshine?" Reckless isn't usually my brand of woman.

Neither is intoxicated nor brokenhearted, but this is my Darling. My *wife*. Something my brother and everyone else who toyed with Wednesday seems to have forgotten. For better or worse. In life and beyond death. We belong to each other.

"Please," she whimpers and that's all it takes for my hesitations to crumble.

I drop her onto my shaft, careful not to hurt the woman while her hands search for a part of me to grab onto. She pulls my mouth to her and kisses me again, panting between breaths, begging, "More, please, more."

I back her against the wall and angle myself to drive deeper. She melts into me. If I'm not careful, I'll come soon, and I can't have that until I know my Darling is satisfied.

I rip the front of Darling's dress and drop my lips to her shoulder. Wednesday's back arches and, like a memory come to life, I feel her come undone. When I'm sure she's satisfied, I pull out, set her on her feet, and finish in my hand.

I've already had children and lost them. There is no pain comparable to the feeling, not even death, which is why I won't risk conceiving again. Not even with my Darling. I watch Wednesday in the mirror as I clean myself up. She stands, unmoved from her spot on the wall, eyes closed.

"Yeh okay over there, Sunshine?"

She smiles, still lost in whatever thought has captured her mind, and says, "Yeah. Best I've been in years." She sniffles, then looks down at her feet and wipes her eyes. "If only this were real."

I dry my washed hands on my pants and cross in front of her. She's so tiny, even in heels. She barely reaches my chin. I crouch to be at eye level and try to read what's going on. Wednesday looks older. Tired. So much like the woman I met in the cove, but different too. "How long has it been since yeh left Neverland?"

Wednesday's eyes snap open as her head tilts to the side like she's finally breaking through the fog and seeing me for the first time. "You know about Neverland?"

"Answer me, beautiful. How long?"

"Three years."

Fuck. I run my hands through my hair and push the strands back. It's longer than I like, but the damned things grow faster in this world than they do in mine. I could cut it tonight and by tomorrow it would be in my eyes again. That should have been my first clue that time doesn't run parallel to Neverland. It skips days. Hours. Weeks.

No wonder the Darling looks so lost.

"Why are you here?" Wednesday asks as if she doesn't trust her own eyes.

I don't blame her. I can't begin to imagine the hell she's been through living on these lands. All the more reason to bring her home.

Wednesday tries to cover herself, but the torn dress and her lack of bra leave her chest out there for the world to see. I pull my shirt over my head and hand it to her. Can't have everyone looking at what's mine while we make our way to the ship.

"I owe yeh a voyage, love. Thought yeh could use a ride back home."

Wednesday's eyes dart to her date, still out cold from the bit of dust I stole from Belle on the floor. "What about him?"

I walk over and tuck the man's cock back into his pants. Despite trying to claim what was never his, he's done me no wrong and doesn't deserve to be shamed by being left exposed. I check his pulse to make sure I didn't hit him with too much magic and am satisfied when I feel the slow beat steadily quickening beneath my fingertips.

"He'll wake before sunrise." I pause, giving her time to process, then add, "Yeh should cover yehself."

"Oh." She pulls my forgotten shirt over her head. It falls to her thighs, nearly as long as her dress. Her gaze drifts to the mark on my shoulder and the deep purple trails that have spread like veins across my skin. "Are you going to be okay?"

In truth? I'm not sure, but Bell's poison and my well-being aren't something worth troubling the Darling with. We have enough on our plates navigating to the ship tonight and the voyage back to Neverland tomorrow won't be easy.

I force a grin and extend my hand, which she quickly takes. It feels good having her close again. Almost like old times. Too bad I know it can't last. "With yeh by my side, Sunshine, I've never been better."

CHAPTER 14

"Stop," Wednesday gasps, her voice strained. "I can't go any further." She doubles over, her hands bracing against her knees. Shallow, rapid breaths do little to alleviate the burning sensation in her chest.

We've walked ten blocks tonight, across the street and along the waterway. We're close to Father's old building. The names of the roads may have changed, and the structures are different, but the river stays the same, as does the bridge. The four walls I slaved in may not be here anymore, but I'd know their location all the same.

Wednesday's gaze finds a spot of land that, decades ago, had a bench overlooking the channel. She stares at it, almost puzzled, and I wonder if she remembers all the afternoons we spent having lunch there. It was our thing, every Thursday at noon. A ritual Wendy started once Father announced our arranged engagement, a way for us to get to know each other.

I learned she was allergic to peanut butter and hated chocolate. Her favorite fruit was strawberries and she favored cats over dogs because of their independence. She'd rather have her hair up in a ponytail than down, but feared her hairline would recede. She hated makeup, but her mother would chastise her for leaving the house without it, so she wore as little as possible. And how her favorite flower was the carnation. Yellow. Not pink.

As for Wendy, she learned every secret I ever had.

"We've got only about a mile to go."

"A mile?" Wednesday's eyes widen in disbelief. She stands

straight and tries to look commanding, but her shoulders round forward and her face falls. She's exhausted. Rightly so after the night I've given her. "You're asking a lot of a drunk girl in heels."

Perhaps I am. This world doesn't lend itself to walking. Cars crowd the roads and planes dirty up the skies. In Neverland, we walk or sail. A two-mile trek is nothing more than time spent on the journey, but I get the feeling that walking more than a block is unusual in this world. The Darling's shoes are less than ideal, too. I imagine traveling on a three-inch spike would be difficult, which could be why she's steadily gotten slower. If I were alone, I'd have been back to the boat by now.

"Put yeh arms around me," I order. Time is ticking away. We need to set sail before the sun rises if we're to make it to the tip of the Triangle by daybreak tomorrow. If we miss the full moon, we'll have to wait another month for the portal to open again. I'm not sure Neverland has that much time left. The pirates need me and the Lost...

They have Peter, although I get the feeling that if he left the Darling here this long, something is amiss.

Wednesday obeys and lets me lift her into my arms without questioning or complaining. The stitches on my back stretch as the muscles bend to adjust to her weight. The sensation isn't pleasant, but it's not the worst pain I've felt as of late, either.

"You're hurt," she says, careful not to touch Belle's bite mark. "You shouldn't be carrying me."

"Yehr as light as air. I'll be fine." I'm not exaggerating. She's like paper in my arms. Thin and fragile.

This world has not been kind to the Darling and I want to know why. I want to understand what she's been through the last few years and why she was so damn reckless at that bar. If she truly thinks I'm a memory brought to life in the night, then someone needs to have a talk with her about boundaries. Life is meant to be lived, with a nominal amount of danger thrown into the mix, not risked for moments of pleasure or memories lost in a black void.

"You know they make this thing called a car," she says as we near the bridge. "We can easily get a ride to wherever it is you want to go."

"I'm not meant to be in the world, Sunshine, or any of its contraptions." Also, the motorwagons look a lot different than the last time I saw, let alone rode in, one. I don't like how they entrap their passengers. Yeh can't feel the air on yehr cheeks or smell the spring blooms as yeh drive by. They shut yeh away from the world and that's not a vessel I want to be trapped in.

"Wish I could say the same," she mumbles. Her sorrow is heartbreaking. She stares into the night, falling into her mind again. I can see I'm losing her, and I'm not ready to let go.

"Peter was right to bring yeh to this world but wrong to leave yeh on yehr own, which is why I'm taking yeh home."

She hums once in agreement, but I'm not sure my words are getting through. It's ok, though. Everything will be alright once she wakes in the morning and realizes I'm here for her.

I hold Wednesday a little tighter, hoping she can sense how grateful I am to have found her, even if having her this close is a bitter pill. The last time I had Wendy in my arms like this was on our wedding night. I carried her from the car to our hotel room. We laughed as I struggled to climb three flights of stairs, then fell into each other for the rest of the evening once I made it to our room. Tonight seems to have unwound itself backward, starting with sex and ending in my arms, but I don't mind. I thought Belle had stolen these memories from me. To have the Darling in my arms again is a gift I won't question.

Wednesday rests her head against my chest and closes her eyes. Her breaths are deep and steady. Peaceful. "I wish that were true. It's going to hurt when you leave."

"What hurts yeh, Sunshine?"

"Feeling hollow again." Her words grow softer as she drifts off to sleep, "I thought I'd see Mira tonight, but this is nice, too."

"Who's Mira?" I ask, but Wednesday is out cold. I let her

sleep. Reckoning that I'll find that answer in the morning. We have a long journey ahead of us tonight and an even bigger one tomorrow.

❧

"THAT HER?" SMEE ASKS, HER EYEBROWS ARCHING, SEEMINGLY unimpressed by the tiny unconscious woman in my arms. Or perhaps it's how Wednesday is wearing my shirt and I'm tending to her in a way I have no other.

I step into the rowboat waiting for us on the River Thames and settle myself in the seat, careful not to wake Wednesday. Smee shoves us off the bank and then grabs the oars. She rows us, knowing good and well that I wouldn't bring just any mortal back to the ship.

"I hope she was worth it," Smee adds, and I can't help but note the jealousy in her tone.

Smee and I have never been anything more than captain and first mate. There may have been a few longing stares on both ends, but my body has been Belle's for what feels like an eternity, while my heart has only ever belonged to my wife. There's never been room for anyone else. "She is."

Smee rows silently to the ship. This is one thing I've always appreciated about her. She doesn't feel the need to fill the quiet spaces with drivel. If she speaks it's purposeful, occasionally thoughtful, but never for the sake of simply making noise. "Your bite mark looks like shit. Why didn't you tell me the poison was spreading?"

I glance down at the deep purple marks on my chest. The veins have spread to my arm and nearly reach my elbow. If not for the festering hole, it could pass for a terrible tattoo of a jellyfish. Oddly enough, the tentacles stretching toward my heart aren't as vibrant as they once were. Their length stretches across my chest, but instead of being a deep maroon, they've faded to a soft purple. "It wasn't high on my priorities. Getting the Darling was."

Her brows wrinkle with disapproval. "You've never tried to find her before. Why now?"

"The Island changed when she arrived and it changed again when she left." I didn't notice it at first. The shifts were subtle. Birds in the sky. Bugs in the air—pretty ones, not just the blood-suckers. Things that lay sleeping woke, but the biggest change was the sun. It rose for the first time since we arrived in Never-land and that had *everything* to do with Wednesday. I'm not sure how or why just yet, but I'll figure it out. "I think the Darling might be the key to breaking Belle's timelock on Neverland. I haven't healed yet, which means her dust is weakening."

Smee leans forward, letting the oars rest in their holders. I can see the worry in her eyes. She would have made a good wife and mother to someone had death not selfishly stolen her. Too bad for him, I wanted her, too. "If Belle's dust weakens and your wounds don't heal, you'll die, Cap."

"Good. I'm ready." The tide carries us the last few feet to the port side of the Jolly Roger. Our tiny boat bumps into it and the force is enough to jolt us around a bit. I wonder briefly if this is what it feels like for the souls we pull out of the Neversea. My experience was different. My choice given before I knew what I'd condemned us to.

"You don't mean that." Smee grabs the faded netting hanging over the taffrail of the boat and whistles. Someone from the crew drops a rope ladder over the side. We could have climbed the net, but life is hard enough. Why not do things the easy way when given the chance? "How are we going to get her on the ship? You can't carry her and climb."

"Yehr the brains, Smee. I trust yeh can figure something out." The easiest way would be to hoist Wednesday and me up when we raise the rowboat, but Smee needs to figure that out on her own. If Belle's poison keeps spreading, the Jolly Roger will need a new captain, and Smee is the only one I'd leave her to.

Smee groans loudly, making her point that I would be lost

without her, then smiles. "No chance the Darling can fly, can she?"

Perhaps. There's no telling what gifts the Island graced her with or how far their powers stretch, but until I know for sure what the Darling is capable of I'm keeping all my suspicions to myself. "I think Peter solely holds that card."

"Of course, he does. Your brother is never around when we need him," she grumbles as one of our deckhands lowers the cables down to connect the raft.

"Yeh know why he can't be a part of anything we do." The Fae are tricky. Bargains are never what they seem. There's always more hiding beneath the surface, twists and sacrifices one can never predict. I didn't ask enough questions the day I met Belle. I blindly made a bargain to keep those I loved safe. It took Wendy from this world. It created an unmendable rift with Peter and left me with no one but the Fae bitch herself until she needed new souls and the cove was created.

"You're right. I do." Smee clasps the claw hook around the loop and secures the boat. I smile, pleased she came to the same conclusion I did about the rowboat. I knew she would.

"But does he?" she continues. "Or any of the souls on the Island for that matter? The pirates think he's a monster that's in bed with the Fae, trying to keep them from moving on to the next life. The Lost think you're a heathen, stealing souls for your own diabolical needs. Why not tell everyone the truth and about what you're doing?"

"Yeh know why." Because it's my fault we were all trapped in Neverland. I chartered the ship. I broke course to follow the whispers of legend. I damned us all.

"When are you going to let your guilt go?" Smee steps off the boat and grabs the ladder. She whistles again and the crew hoists Wednesday and me up. "No one in their right mind would have believed the legend to be true. You sought an adventure to excite your boys and woo your wife. Did it go wrong? Yeah, but you don't have to keep punishing yourself."

That's where Smee's wrong. It was my fault. I knew to avoid the Triangle, just like I knew the vortex at its center would take us someplace magical.

I just didn't know everything it would cost me.

Chapter 15

Wednesday

My head is killing me, so much so that the pounding woke me from the deepest sleep I've had in a long time. I don't want to open my eyes. I already know the sun will be mean and the world will be punishing because I let myself fall too deeply down the rabbit hole last night. Even lying still, gravity isn't my friend. My stomach rolls from side to side and I don't know if I'm kicking myself for not eating dinner or grateful.

Last night was something else. Wendy's memories have always been vivid, to the point where sometimes they're all I have of Peter to hold onto, whereas mine from Neverland are broken. I spent so much time angry with him that I don't have many good ones to look back on. As for Shadow, he gave me two nights to remember. Two amazing nights filled with answers and orgasms, but it's not enough to justify the kind of broken heart he left. If it weren't for Wendy and the way her past mingles with the present, I might have moved on by now.

Loving a ghost is painful, improbable, and lonely.

But loving the man Wendy knew, and feeling those moments so fully, it's as if I lived them myself, and that complicates things. Especially when she loved two men with her whole heart. Each in a different way and for different reasons, but it was still love.

Which brings me back to last night.

What the hell was that?

I've had some wildly amazing sex dreams that left me sweaty and panting when I woke, but I've never been intimate with someone and seen another man's face. Out of all my Neverland lovers, I thought it would be Peter since he and I have actually had sex before. To see James was crazy. Unexpected.

But fuck, it felt good.

I don't know if I was drugged or just drunk, but to feel something besides emptiness again was worth waking up on the right side of the Grim Reaper's hangover-blade.

"Pretend all you want," an unfamiliar female voice says, "but I know you're awake."

A surge of panic has me hoping that I didn't let that man bring me back to his place. Logically, he had to have, unless we invited a third person into my bed that I don't recall. Stars above, if this is his wife I think I might cry. I know what it feels like to have your man betray your trust. I never want to be that source of pain for another woman.

The first thing I see when I open my eyes is wood planking, running laterally along the wall. I push myself up, noticing how it surrounds the room and how little decorative elements there are. The space is the size of an average bedroom, but there is no dresser or TV. No closet or noticeable bathroom. There's only the bed, large enough to comfortably fit three, and a chest at its foot.

And the girl.

Can't forget her.

"I see why Cap likes you." She frowns disapprovingly. "You're pretty, but I'm not convinced you were worth the hassle."

"Cap?" I ask, trying to figure out what the nickname could be short for and come up with nothing. Maybe it's short for some ethnic name that matches his heritage. Last night's lover was African... I think. Or maybe Hattian. Am I a terrible person for not knowing?

"Hmm. Not too bright, though," she says more to herself than me.

"Look, I don't know who you are, but if you're his wife, then I am so sorry. I didn't know about you and wouldn't have slept with Cap if I did," I insist, my guilt eating away at me.

Have I really sunk so low as to become this person? The fear that Tyle is right—that I need to move on and stop blindly searching for a lead that will never come—knocks the wind out of me.

I don't want to give up.

I'm not ready to move on.

But letting my morals slide to try and fill an endless void isn't something I'm okay with. Living my life out of a suitcase and chasing ghosts isn't healthy either. I know I have to make a change. I'm just not ready.

"Quit giving the girl a hard time, will yeh, Smee?"

That voice. I recognize it the second James opens his mouth. I look past the girl, Smee, and jump out of bed as soon as I see him. He welcomes me, wrapping his arms around my waist, and pulls me in for a suffocating hug.

I breathe him in, relishing the thick scent of seawater and pine. I never thought I'd see anyone from Neverland again, especially James. I pull back and touch his face, just to be sure I'm not imagining him. His day-old whiskers are rough on my hands, but the coarseness reminds me that he's real.

"You're here," I say in disbelief.

"Aye. I am."

It hits me then that last night wasn't a crazy dream or warped hallucination. I slept with two men last night, one being the brother of the other half of my soul. *Oh, my stars. Peter is going to kill me!*

I jump out of James's arms and use his shirt to cover myself. I feel terrible. How could I? How could he?

"Smee, I think yeh should leave," he says to the girl.

She crosses her arms and gives him a Cheshire grin. "I don't know, Cap. This is starting to get good." James narrows his eyes at her and she groans. "Fine. I'll go see what Cook's got going for breakfast."

Smee walks past us, chuckling under her breath. She looks at me with those judgy eyes and my belly twists. I get the feeling that she knows exactly what I let James do to me last night, and I don't think she's happy about it.

Smee closes the door to the cabin and I snap my hand up to smack James across the face. He catches my wrist, one lip lifting in bemusement.

"Careful, Sunshine. Yehr going start a game I'm not certain yeh want to play yet."

I jerk my hand back so unbelievably angry with him. And myself. And turned on. Why am I turned on? My center tingles with anticipation. My needy vag wants him. Hell, I want him and I can't explain why. I bite my lip, whispering to Wendy's feelings to go away, but it appears that she wants him to.

"Why are you here?" I ask, unsure if I should push him out the door or push my way back into his arms.

Wendy was a confused woman, forced to choose one man over the other, never fully satisfied with either. I don't know how. Peter was gentle and eager to satisfy me, not caring about himself. Pan was wild, desperate to feel what he never could.

But James, he was something else.

"I promised yeh a voyage." His gaze skirts the walls of the cabin for a moment, then finds me again. "Seeing as yeh found yehr way to Florida on yehr own, I thought a return expedition might make up for my shortcomings."

His comings were anything but short, if I remember correctly.

Stars above, I'm such a slut. But I don't care.

I grab James by the back of the neck and pull him to me. He is ready, waiting for my invitation, and doesn't hold back the second it comes. He rips open the shirt I'm wearing and finds my chest. His fingers touch, and kneed, and pinch and by the stars, it feels good. He guides me backward until my knees find the edge of the bed and our kiss breaks as I fall onto it.

I watch James as he pulls his shirt off, too consumed by the vision in front of me to feel guilty. He's beautiful. His body is corded with more muscle than both Peter's or Pan's. Dark marks stretch from a wound on his neck across his chest and down his arm. They fold into the dips and grooves of his body, looking like they belong, but something about them feels wrong. I don't get to ask what they are because James pulls my legs open and dips his head between them.

My panties are an afterthought and must have been lost last night because I don't know where they are. I gasp the moment his tongue meets my folds and reach for the sheets. My instinct is to pull away and fight the pleasure I desperately crave but James holds me there until I'm shaking with a release that feels so good it coats the bed.

He licks his lips, hungrily looking for more of my juices, and kisses my inner thigh.

I want more.

Need more.

I curl those long dark locks around my fingers and push his head back between my legs. He chuckles and the vibration of his laugh is intoxicating. I should feel guilty face-fucking my ex-lover's brother, but his tongue and his fingers feel too good for me to care. I come again, although I'm not sure how it's possible because every man I've been with since Mira's birth has fallen short, yet here James is bringing me to my knees twice within minutes.

He kisses my inner thigh once more as I lay on his bed, my heart racing, gasping for air.

"Now that I've had my breakfast," he says coyly, "we should probably head downstairs for yours."

James's thick length taunts me through his trousers. There's no way I'm letting him out of this room like that. Everyone will know what we've done if they don't already.

And I don't like the way that Smee woman looks at him.

"What I want isn't downstairs." I roll onto my knees and grab James's hips. He raises an eyebrow at me as I unfasten his pants, but he doesn't stop me. He's not a gentleman like Cass, wanting to preserve my virtue or whatever. James lets me take what I want without question, and what I want is to choke on his dick.

I fist his shaft and pump it a few times to get it ready. I like the way it feels, his skin to mine. A glistening bead of precum stares me down and I've never wanted to taste someone's cock as much as I want his. I lick the head, relishing the sweet tanginess of his pre-seed, then swallow as much of him as my throat can handle. I take almost half of him before my swallow reflex kicks in.

Not gag. I don't have one of those.

James grabs me by the hair and guides me to a pace that suits him. I bob up and down, slurping and sucking, anxiously waiting for the moment I can taste him. My nipples pebble again, my body wanting more. He senses my desire and pulls my hair harder. I grab James's balls and apply pressure to that sweet spot near his taint. He wants to play dirty, I can, too.

"Godsdamn yeh, woman," he groans a moment before filling my mouth.

I suck every last drop out of him, happy to have provided even an ounce of the pleasure he gave me.

And then feel like a horrible person again. The fucking whiplash is brutal. Guilt gnaws at my conscience as his taste lingers on my tongue. I can't do that again, no matter how good it felt. It's wrong and disrespectful to Peter, not that I've seen or heard from him in three years...

Does he even have a say in my life anymore?

Stop it, Wednesday! Morals. You have those. Remember?

"What just happened?" I ask, trying to piece together the bits I understand...which isn't much.

"It's called oral. Do we need the sex talk, Sunshine?" James teases as he pulls up his pants.

"Not what I meant." I look for the shirt I wore last night and find it in a heap by the bed, buttons scattered across the floor. It's going to be about as useful as my dress.

James, the perceptive one that he is, opens the trunk at the foot of the bed and tosses a pair of sweatpants and a baggy tee at me. "Ah. Yeh want to know why whenever we're in a room it's like lightning in a bottle."

"Not exactly how I'd put it, but yeah."

"Yehr my wife," he says as if that's all the answer I need.

I strip out of what's left of my clothes and step into his. A drawstring keeps the pants from falling off my waist, but the shirt swallows me. I feel like I'm back in college, wearing Kenny's clothes after a wild night. All I'm missing is some cold pizza, a walk of no shame, and a hangover.

I hold up my left hand and teasingly wiggle my fingers. "Where's my ring, honey?"

James bends over the trunk again and rummages through it. I watch him, fascinated by the muscles of his back. Curious about the scars and stitches. Desperate too...

For stars' sake, Wednesday! Get it together!

"If it's a ring yeh want." He holds up a diamond the size of my thumbnail. It's beautiful and sparkling, set on a white gold band, and literally the ring I have always dreamed of. "Then it's a ring yeh'll get."

My heart races. I feel like a kid on Christmas looking at all the presents, anxious to open them and start playing. Until the logical side of my mind slaps me upside the head. That is probably Wendy's ring. Not mine. And even if it was meant for me, I'm not ready for whatever it is James has to offer.

I take a step back and shake both my hands. James is too much, and moving way too fast. I've literally met the man what... three times? Two of those times in the past twenty-four hours. "Easy, killer. I was kidding. "

He chuckles and tucks the ring back into its holder. "As was I, but also...not. Our vows explicitly said in this life and beyond. That lust yeh feel." He comes closer and brushes his fingers down my arm. "The insatiable need to jump my bones." He links his hand with mine and brings my knuckles to his lips. "That is this world giving us her blessing again."

I shake my head, trying to push away a new fog of desire. If I didn't know any better, I'd say we were back in Neverland already because being there intensified everything I felt, both good and bad. But I can feel the literal weight of this world pulling down on me. It anchors me to the moment while pushing me toward him all the same. "Wendy is Peter's soulmate. I belong to him."

"A soul is meant to love millions. It fractures and splits to give itself away over and over again, but it only has one life mate." James's lips curl into a sad smile, and I feel the weight of his suffering. He knew how much Wendy loved Peter, how potent her feelings are for him that run through me, and still he fights for even a chance at there being an *us*. "Love is always a choice. I chose my wife knowing her heart was torn, and she chose me. Yeh are not Wendy, Sunshine. Yeh can forge yer own path in whatever way yeh see fit. I will be by yer side, wherever it may lead. That is my blessing and burden as her husband."

I open my mouth, unsure of what to say. Last night I went to bed a hollow version of myself, desperate to find my way back to Mira. Today I woke with a fighting chance of reaching her and feeling like a human again, ready to move on and stop loving a ghost. It's crazy. Impractical.

And so fucking confusing.

My stomach growls, breaking the tension of the moment. James chuckles and says, "Seems I wasn't able to satiate all yer hunger." He kisses my blushing cheek and drapes his arm over my shoulder. "Come on, Sunshine. Let's get yeh fed. We have a grand voyage ahead of us."

CHAPTER 16
Wednesday

Walking into the galley is like being the new girl at school all over again. Everyone looks at me, their eyes judging me for wearing James's clothing. Their faces tight, letting me know, without question, that I was not expected.

All of which makes me painfully self-conscious.

James slips his hand in mine and a man with a fishhook as an earring arches his bushy brown eyebrow. That man shakes his head and then goes back to eating a piece of toast with jelly.

"Crew," James says in his ish-accent. I still don't know where it stems from, but now that I've traveled and spent the last year in England, it doesn't feel English to me. "This is Wednesday. She'll be joining us on our voyage back to Neverland."

"Why?" another crewmate, with woven dreadlocks that reach his back, asks. There are eight people at the table. A total of ten crew members, if I count James and Smee. "She's alive with the world at her feet." The man cocks his head and narrows his eyes at me. "What's so shitty about your life that you'd give it all up for eternal damnation?"

"Rodgers!" Smee snaps. Her voice is commanding, and by the reaction everyone gives to her outburst, I'd say she's earned the respect of the men in this room. "We don't question the captain. Remember?"

"Aye," Rodgers says, begrudgingly.

James leads us to the other side of the small space and motions for me to join him near the head of the table to a seat that looks like it belongs to Smee. I get the feeling that skipping line in the pecking order isn't going to do me any favors. I've already been thrown off a boat once. Re-living that experience is not high on my to-do list.

"I'm not hungry. I think I'll just go back to my—"

"Sit, new girl," Smee insists.

There's a murmured chuckle somewhere to my right, but I don't know which crew member made the sound, and James seems uninterested. So, I let it go. This is a pick-your-battle situation, and a little laughter at my expense isn't worth challenging a pirate over. If the stories are true, they should be ruthless sword fighters. Whereas I have never even been in a fistfight.

The breakfast spread is simple—scrambled eggs, toast, and sausage—but there's enough of it to feed an army. Everyone's plates are full, with some reaching for more. I watch as everyone, Smee included, eats more in this sitting than I do in a day. It's fascinating the way they almost inhale their food. A strange thought drags my mind to a pirate movie I saw in high school, and I can't help but wonder if their other needs are also insatiable. Before James, no one—man or woman—had been able to satisfy my physical needs. But what if the dead's curse runs deeper? What if they are always hungry? Always longing for the affection of another? Always wanting something they can never have?

"Eat." James sets a platter of food in front of me and it's more than I can finish.

I stare at it, wide-eyed, unsure of where to start. My stomach is rolling, possibly from the motion of the ocean. Possibly from the alcohol I drank last night. Whatever the reason, the only thing that looks the slightest bit appetizing is the bread. "This is too much."

"The crew doesn't stop for lunch," he says as he makes himself a jelly and egg sandwich. "Yehr next meal won't be until dusk. Fill yehr belly while you can, love."

Looking at all the food makes me nauseous, but I nod and eat as much as I can. Even if I were feeling fabulous, I'm not used to stuffing my face like this. I thrive on multiple small meals a day. A snack here. A coffee there. A bagel or whatever floats my fancy here. I eat and eat and barely manage to get a quarter of my plate cleaned before my stomach is bloated and hurting.

"I can't," I say, leaning back into the wooden chair. "I'm done."

All the other crew members have already left. It's just James and I alone in the galley. He chuckles and reaches for a slice of toast, the fourth out of six on my plate. "I'll have Ben put this on ice for you. Yeh'll be wanting it later."

"How does someone who looks like you eat so much?"

He clasps his hands over his stomach and grins. "I burn the calories. Want me to show yeh how?" He winks.

My cheeks flush and I don't know why. That man has already seen and had more of my body than I ever thought possible, but my mind strays. It mixes Wendy's past with the last twenty-four hours and I am ashamed to admit I want to know if he can make me feel good again. I press my lips together, a smile lifting them, then pretend to be annoyed as I say. "You're insufferable."

"Perhaps, but a small part of yeh loves it."

I do. And I hate myself for it. "What's the plan, James? Why am I here?"

"That's the million-dollar question," Smee says, emerging from the shadows. "What is the plan, Cap? We can't go back the way we came. The rules are different with a beating heart. You know this."

"Dammit. Do I have to die again? I was really hoping there was another way."

"What?" James looks at me, shocked. "No. Of course not. Wait... again?"

"I can't swim. Peter pushed me off a boat," I say with a shrug like it's no big deal when really being at the mercy of the ocean again has me more than a little freaked out.

"Fucking hell." James runs a hand through his hair and pushes back the long strands that have fallen into his eyes. "We need to work on teaching you then."

I find the tassels of my sweatpants and twist the strands between my fingers. I've tried to learn, countless times, and it always ends the same. The moment my head goes underwater, I panic. I can't help it, and believe me, I've tried everything. I even tried learning to doggy paddle with my head above the water like little kids do. My ass sinks like lead and, even though my arms move, it's like they invite the water instead of moving it. I'm hopeless.

"It's not a bad idea," Smee says. "Then she'll be one of us."

"I'm not a murderer and she's not dying," James says, his tone final.

"Pa...Peter said that the Bermuda Triangle is a gateway. Ships get lost there all the time. We might have a shot at making it through the barrier under the full moon tonight." I've also tried this already, but maybe James's ship will be different. This boat has already crossed the barrier between their world and this one once. My rental from Bob's Boat Yard had never seen a speck of Neverland magic and did nothing but run out of gas.

James gives me a look that sends my tummy butterflies a flight. I've seen it before, only I can't recall where, and I wonder if it stems from a memory Wendy had locked away. He reaches for a necklace tucked beneath his shirt and opens the small pouch. He holds a golden acorn, sparkling like a glitter-covered craft project my students used to make, only instead of being coated with specks of plastic, it's covered in gold dust.

I shiver as a chill takes hold of me. The sensation is like walking into a standing freezer. Goosebumps pepper every inch of exposed skin. Something deep inside me recognizes the acorn. I wish I knew why.

"Tell me, Sunshine," he says with a wicked grin. "What's yehr happy thought?"

CHAPTER 17

Wednesday

What's my happy thought?

Now that's the question of the day because it can't be *just* a thought. It has to be a memory, something so pure that it resonates to my core. A singular defining moment that carries enough joy to lift this ship literally into space and cross the galaxies.

No pressure.

I pace the space of James's cabin and try to think. There are only a few hours left until sunset. I've spent all day trying to come up with some great moment in my life and I've got nothing. The few tiny moments I've thought of—graduating at the top of my class, earning teacher of the year—they're great, but I don't feel like they're enough.

There's a knock at the door. I stop mid-pace, my heart in my throat. I glance out the window and note that the sun is still up. Time hasn't run away from me yet. At least, I don't think it has. It's hard to tell when there are no clocks, no shadows, and only an endless canvas of blue to look out at.

The person outside knocks again and that second rap has my lips lifting in a smile. There's only one person on this ship I can think of who has the decency to wait for permission before entering. "Come in."

James pops his head in. His dark eyes skim over the room before they find me in the far corner, chewing on my thumbnail. He lets himself into the small space and closes the door behind him, an unassuming smile on his face. "Hello, Sunshine. Yeh've locked yehrself away all day. Are yeh all right?"

90

Agony has me on the brink of tears. How do I tell someone who crossed the barrier between space and time to find me that I am going to let him down? I don't want to talk about me or my happy thought. I don't particularly want to talk about him and Wendy either. I could talk about us... if we are an us. "Why do you call me that?"

"What?" James reaches for the strand of hair that's fallen over my shoulder. He twists it between his fingers, looking one hundred percent at ease with being this close to me. As if us being together doesn't make his heart race or his skin tingle. Or like it's not a constant struggle to look me in the eyes instead of at my lips.

He seems perfectly fine.

Whereas I am a complete mess. "Sunshine. Everyone else calls me *the Darling.*"

"Ah." James walks to a wall at the side of the room and presses his palm to the lateral siding. A hidden door releases and swings outward. He tugs on a sliding shelf, opens it all the way, and exposes an old polyphon. He winds the handle and adjusts the needle so a pleasant melody can play. "Dance with me."

I laugh because, of course, he wants to dance while I'm having a minor freakout. Why wouldn't he? And even though I feel overwhelmed and anxious, and I know that feeling his skin on mine again will be a mistake, I take his hand and let him guide us into an eighth-grade-style sway. We take tiny steps, from side to side, not able to spread out due to the lack of space.

"Wendy Darling was a shooting star in the sky. Beautiful but utterly unreachable to Peter. He gazed upon her with wonder, never satisfied with the pieces of her he got." James spins me once, then pulls me tight against his chest, his hard muscles pressing against my soft skin. "For me, Wendy was the center of life. My world revolved around her happiness and I basked in the smiles I earned, but yeh were an unexpected ray of light in the darkness that had consumed me. Yeh are everything Wendy was, but brighter. The shining light I gravitate toward, even though I know my chances of being burned are high."

"Sunshine," I say, unable to fight my smile. These Neverland men and their riddles. I've never met anyone else who could wrap a compliment in such pretty words while still making me wonder, "*What the hell are they saying?*"

"I never liked being called *Darling,* but I don't mind Sunshine." I press my head to James's chest and listen to the music. Like Cass and the Lost, he has no heartbeat, but that doesn't scare me like it used to. James is living and breathing. He is as real as the sun in the sky and the wood under my feet.

"Yehr struggling with a happy thought," he says without a hint of judgment in his tone.

I bite my bottom lip and look down at my feet. The shame of failing is almost as bad as the embarrassment. "Is it that obvious?"

"We would be flying right now if yeh weren't." More facts. Not judgment, but the truth hurts. I could be halfway to holding my daughter again if I weren't such a failure.

"Oh." I step out of James's arms and hug myself. I don't know what to say. I had a good upbringing with two parents who loved me. Nothing tragic happened to me—besides dying at the hands of a living legend—and I didn't live a miserable life. But I didn't have anything *great* happen to me either.

Mira's birth should have been the best day of my life, but it turned into the worst when Cass stole her.

I've loved one mortal man, but all of my memories with him are tainted because he cheated on me and married my sister.

And any happy moments I could have had with Peter or Cass are stained with lies, murder, and distrust.

I *really* need to do a better job at picking who I give my heart to. At that thought, my gaze drifts to James's face again. His lips curl into a sympathetic smile and I think back to the time we've spent together. It hasn't been much, but from what I can tell he hasn't tried to manipulate or hurt me even once. Which is more than I can say for the other Neverland men.

"Yehr overthinking this, Sunshine." He reaches up and cups my cheek. "Relax."

"Easy for you to say. No one is counting on you to power a flying ship."

"True, but everyone here expects me to guide it and keep them safe." James walks to the edge of the bed and sits. He moves his pillow aside and then taps the mattress. "How's bout I tell yeh one of mine?"

I find a space beside him and cross my legs. Peter never talked about the past, and Pan was more interested in me than all things Wendy. Since being back in this world, I've seen so much through her eyes. Her memories almost feel like mine, but they are only one side of the story. Her life is a book with the back of each page missing. I don't have the context or background for the visions my dreams give me. I'm piecing together the pages of her life, but I don't know if they're in order or what bits might be missing.

"I knew Wendy Darling loved Peter. Hell, everyone knew. Yeh could tell from the time they were kids that she was enamored by him."

"This doesn't sound very happy, James."

He chuckles and takes my hand. His fingers trail along the thin lines on my palm, both tickling and soothing the skin. "I didn't care. She was a child, six years younger than me, and I was set on making my father proud. While Peter played in the trees, I was shadowing Father to learn the business. He was in the finance industry, and as the eldest son, it was my duty to follow in his footsteps. When I was eighteen, I was drafted into the war. Wendy was twelve, not even a woman yet but, even then, she was kind. She wrote me letters while I was away, mostly because her father made her, but eventually, we forged a friendship. It was platonic in every sense. She would tell me things about her life she couldn't tell anyone else, ask me questions she was too shy to voice to her family, and I would tell her about the places I'd traveled."

Flickers of Wendy's memories flash through my mind. I see her hand excitedly penning letters and feel her heart race when a new one came. What started as a chore turned into an unexpected friendship. But James was right. That's all it was. I don't sense any romantic inclinations when she reads what he wrote her.

"I knew the moment Peter had won her heart." James's smile falls. "I was due to return home in the fall and months had passed since my last letter. I wrote her every week up until I got my notice of discharge and not once did she write me back. It hurt more than I expected. Wendy had become a constant in my world where not even the next day was guaranteed and without warning, she was gone."

I close my fingers and hold his hand in mine. I feel this memory too, only from Wendy's point of view there wasn't just sorrow but also guilt. Understanding firsthand what abandonment feels like, I sympathize with the pain James must have felt and hate knowing what she put him through. "You don't have to keep going. It's okay."

He chuffs out a breath but continues. "Wendy Darling stood beside Peter, her hands delicately folded in front of her when the driver brought me back to my familial home. She had blossomed from the little girl I left behind into a woman as beautiful as the sun is bright. I was so excited to see her, but she acted as if the last five years we'd written to each other never happened. We were strangers and, unbeknownst to us, about to be engaged." James stands and walks to the window. He stares out at the sea, watching the sun's darkening rays glitter against the rolling waves.

His words pull at memories buried deep in my soul. I find that day in Wendy's archives, too, buried beneath layers of guilt and despair. She was also excited to see James. So much so that it threw her off guard. He was the brother to the man she'd sworn her heart to, someone completely forbidden, yet he summoned an excitement that outshined anything she'd experienced. She was confused. Didn't know how to act and decided putting a wall between them would be best.

And then life threw a curveball at her she wasn't ready for.

"My homecoming dinner was a disaster," James finally says. "Peter threw his glass of wine across the table when Father made the announcement that he'd arranged for Wendy and me to wed. My brother stormed out of the room, leaving his shaking lover behind. I remember being torn because a part of me wanted to respect Peter's feelings and rebuke the engagement, but I was so jealous of the way Wendy looked at him. I wanted to know what it felt like to be someone's whole world."

"Did she ever make you feel that way?" I know the answer before I even ask the question, but I want so badly for him to have felt that kind of love, even if she didn't.

"Wendy tried. Later that week, she arranged a candlelit dinner on our rooftop under the stars. She wanted to make her parents proud and so she agreed to the marriage. That dinner was her peace offering and our chance at a blank slate. It was our beginning, but not her and Peter's end."

I've seen the night he's talking about, more than once over the years. The moon was so big in the sky, the stars so bright, Wendy thought she could count them all if she tried. There wasn't a single cloud to cast a shadow, and she felt that it was a good omen. She was so nervous, torn between running away as Peter suggested and staying to try and make things work. She knew she could be happy with James. He was a good person with a kind heart. Marrying him would secure the merger her father needed and provide stability for the whole family.

Whereas a life with Peter would tear her family apart. She'd be alone in the world, living like a pauper. She feared love wouldn't be enough to get them through the hard times, and that doubt was enough to make her want to stay.

"She kissed me that night." James touches his lips and laughs under his breath. "I was so nervous I almost botched the whole thing. At twenty-four, I'd had more than my share of lovers, but holding Wendy in my arms that night was nothing short of magic. I fell in love, right then, and knew I'd do anything to make her happy."

"She's your happy thought."

He nods. "My happy thought. My damning thought. She was my everything."

I realize all I've ever wanted was to be someone's happy thought. I didn't even know that could be a relationship goal, but now that I know what it is—when I find someone worthy of trying to fall in love again—I want it. "I don't have a love like that. I don't have anything."

"That, Sunshine, is where yehr wrong." James strides to me and threads his fingers through the hair at the base of my neck. His head dips and his lips brush against mine. "Yeh could have it all. All yeh need is to ask. Ask me to love yeh. Ask me to be yehr happy thought."

I close my eyes, waiting for a kiss that doesn't come. "That's a lot of commitment. What if I'm not ready?"

"I'll wait for yeh. I'll share yeh. I'll do whatever yeh need, but yeh have to explicitly tell me what yeh want."

What I want is an impossibility in this world, but so should be James's existence. By the laws of logic, I shouldn't want a man more than a hundred years my senior. I shouldn't feel guilt tied to another's past. I shouldn't believe in magic, but I do. And while I don't have a happy thought I believe in everything. I just hope it's enough. "I want you to take me to Neverland."

"How?" James asks, his breath warm on my cheeks.

"I want your ship to fly me there. I want to arrive in one piece, and I—"

James's lips crash against mine. We fall backward onto the bed again as the ship jolts beneath us. He ignores the deep swaying of the ocean, solely focusing on me. His hands glide up my shirt as his mouth begins to worship me.

James's hands are heaven. His lips a sinful delight from hell. He's everything I want and shouldn't have wrapped up into one delicious package. He kisses his way down my stomach, removing my sweatpants along the way.

I try to focus on the pleasure, but my mind keeps circling back to the unfinished sentence. There's an urge I can't explain, begging me to finish. I can't relax until I whisper, "And I want my daughter back."

CHAPTER 18

Wednesday

"Cap!" Smee shouts.

I recognize her voice through the haze of lust and wish she would go away. I don't want this to stop. I think I might be addicted to how good James makes me feel.

His fingers dig into my thighs as his tongue ventures as deep inside me as it can possibly go. He gives me everything and nothing at once because all I want is more.

More pleasure.

More of him.

Just. More.

Smee pounds on the door over and over again, demanding James pry his attention from me to her. At this moment, I hate her and I can't say that about many people.

He groans, just as irritated as I am, and yells, "Not now!"

"Captain!" Smee fires back with a sense of urgency. Something is wrong. There's no arguing that whatever it is probably demands the *Captain's* attention. But I wish he didn't have to go.

James holds up one finger and wipes his mouth with the back of his hand. He stomps over to the door loud enough that if there was any question as to if he's annoyed it's been answered. I reach for the thin white blanket that lays across the mattress as he yanks the door open. "Something better be on fucking fire because I said— "

"We're airborne," Smee cuts in with as little emotion as possible. She looks past James to me as I try to cover myself with his bedsheet. There's a fire in her eyes that makes me wonder if Smee is going to be a problem for us. I hope not, but I've got this feeling I can't shake that something bad is coming and pray that it's not by her hands.

"Good," James says as if he expected as much and couldn't care less. He pushes the door closed, but Smee sticks the toe of her heeled black boot in the frame before it can latch shut.

"Don't you think you ought to get out here and guide us?" she counters as she shoves her way into his quarters. "No one has seen you in hours. The crew is spooked. She's a distraction and you are never distracted."

Hours? That's not possible. We were just talking for a few minutes before he and I...

I twist the fabric around myself and tuck an end between my chest, creating a makeshift toga-style dress. There aren't many steps to the window and I can see it's not bright outside anymore, but the thought of losing time again is chilling. It makes me question if my mind is slipping again and that doubt is unnerving.

A never-ending span of darkness sprinkled with little specks of light surrounds us. From my vantage point, there is no up or down. Just an endless night.

Or is this a void like the one I'd fallen into before? Has all of this been a dream? Am I still trapped in the in-between from when Cass spiked my drink?

I try to take a breath, but the air is sticky and hot. It fills my lungs while leaving them painfully hollow. I search for more and more oxygen, trying to find some sense of normalcy while my thoughts spin out of control, but even an easy breath is out of reach.

What if it is a dream? What if I never made it out of the ocean after I fell and this is some wicked version of hell? All I've ever wanted was to be loved and in this fucked up afterlife, love has been taken from me at every turn.

My stomach twists and a knot lodges itself in my throat as the theory sinks its claws in me. No one knows what happens after we die. We could be reborn or simply cease to exist. We could be stuck in a nightmare where nothing and everything makes sense all at once and—

Something cold touches my arms. The icy sensation travels to my fingertips and my head whirls. I hear a voice calling my name, but it's so far away and distorted. It tickles my brain, feeling familiar, but it's not strong enough to lift the feeling of dread.

More thoughts push their way into my conscious stream. Whatever this is, wherever I am, I don't know if I can keep going. I'm exhausted and if Mira wasn't real... I don't want to live.

A jolt of energy shocks my system and I'm finally able to fill my chest with a cold breath of air. I suck it in, greedily looking for more, and specks of light fill my vision. Little by little, the room comes back into view. It's the same wood-lined walls and the same oversized window, only I'm not standing anymore. Somehow, I've fallen and James is on his knees in front of me, a worry line forming a wrinkle on his near-perfect face.

"There yeh are." James touches my cheek and I instinctively lean into him. "Yeh fell out on me for a moment. What happened?"

I worry my lip between my teeth. Every thought I had while in the darkness sticks to me. I don't know up from down anymore. Real from imagined. I wonder if this is what the Lost felt like when they died and found Neverland.

I huff out a heavy breath and glance down at my tattoo. Seems like I branded myself as one of them, even before I realized it could be possible.

"Wednesday?" James queries, his voice laden with worry.

"I don't know what's real and what's not anymore," I admit, and the shame of feeling so broken nearly swallows me.

"Yeh feel this?" James takes my hand and presses it to my chest. My heart beats steadily beneath my palm. He waits for me to respond, but my words are caught in my throat. All I can do is nod once, and he says, "Good."

James reaches for something in his back pocket, a modern-style blade with an orange hilt, and flips it open. He takes my hand and presses the tip of his knife to the pad of my finger. I wince and try to pull my hand back, but he holds it tight. "Yeh feel that, don't yeh?"

"Yes." I find my voice again. It's weak and cracks, revealing how fragile I am. I hate it. I hate not knowing where I stand. But mostly, I hate straddling that line between belief and insanity.

"Dreams don't hurt. When yeh wake, yeh feel all the emotions built up in the journey, but dreams. Don't. Hurt. Yeh can't bleed. Yeh can't love. Yeh can't live." James presses my finger to his mouth and kisses the wound. The few drops of blood I lost stain his lips like rouge, but he doesn't lick it away.

"We need to feed yeh." He takes me by the arms and helps me rise to my feet. "Yehr weak, both physically and mentally. Nothing some bread and stew can't fix."

The ship rocks in the sky more than it did at sea, and I loose my balance. James notices and holds me steady. "I'd forgotten how frail the living are. Magic takes a lot out of yeh, Sunshine. We need to be careful not to use too much until yehr ready. It likes balance and will seek payment for every ounce we use."

He shifts to my side and wraps his arm around my waist. I don't want his help. Looking weak around the pirates makes me nervous, especially where Smee is concerned, but the muscles in my legs shake with every step. My body is exhausted and as much as I don't want it, I need James's help.

"I don't have any magic."

Smee opens the double doors that lead out to the deck. She latches the one and then stands beside the other, waiting for us to come out.

"Are yeh sure about that, love?" James winks and then looks up at the sky.

I follow his gaze to an endless span of twinkling stars. The dark void that threw me into a tizzy is filled with rich hues of purple and blue. Streams of deep green and orange connect constellations. And the stars... they're so bright. So unbelievably beautiful. My thoughts may be questionable, but my mind isn't creative enough to make something as intricate as this sky up. It's real. Every tear-filled night, every desperate attempt to go home, all of it was real.

I walk out onto the deck, wanting to see more. James is at my side with every step, his big brown eyes on me while I take in the evening's beauty. I try to find the words to describe the night and the hum beneath my skin but nothing comes close.

It's beyond stunning.

"Are yeh daring enough to look over the taffrail?" James asks.

His hand slips from my waist to my hand and I let him guide us to one side of the boat. He waits for me to levy my stance before placing himself behind me and caging me in with his arms. There's no chance of me falling overboard. He's made sure I feel safe and secure, unlike the last time I found myself in this position.

I grip the wood railing and look down. The same span of darkness that stretches above us floats beneath us. We're flying, somewhere in the depths of space, leaving a trail of golden dust behind us. "It's incredible."

"Yehr incredible."

I spin in James's arms and lean against the railing. He takes a step forward and presses his body against mine. He's not making a move, but taking another wordless action to prove to me I'm safe. Warmth blooms in my chest. This man is the complete opposite of his brother. Protective. Supportive. And honest. He's offered more to me without asking than Peter Pan did combined. "Thank you."

"There's no need to thank me. I haven't done anything worth yeh debt."

"You found me."

"Sunshine, I will always find yeh." He looks into my eyes and I see the depth in his words. In this life and the next. Beyond the constraints of life that not even death can yield, this man is and forever will be mine. "Come. Yeh need to eat and then rest. We'll be in Neverland by sunrise."

I yawn, feeling the fatigue of the night again, despite my excitement.

Tomorrow, I'll be home.

Tomorrow, I will be one step closer to finding my daughter.

CHAPTER 19

Pan

""We'll be safe in here," Emmit says, one hand around Xyris's waist to help him balance.

He woke from Belle's time-stop about a half mile ago and while he is moving, he's groggy and sore. His muscles are fatigued from lack of food and hanging by their arms. Belle's dust may have stopped Xyris from dying of starvation, but it didn't prevent the wear and tear on his body from being held captive.

A strain we all feel.

After an hour of walking through the underground tunnels, Aria finally stirs in my arms. She shifts and her skin sticks to my shirt. She winces and then groans, but as the dust fades away her groans turn into cries, which echo into screams when she fully wakes. Tears fill her eyes as she tries to climb out of my arms, but her legs are weak. She falls to the ground, crying even louder.

My stomach sours. I want so badly for the Island to heal Aria's wounds, just like I wanted it to bring Heidi back from the brink of death, but its magic is still out of reach. The electric hum that should be rolling through my veins is a cold wash of nothingness. The darkness of the cavern won't listen to me. I can't even manage to create a mage light to guide our way through the tunnels. If not for Emmit and his wielding abilities, we'd be stumbling around in the dark because I am utterly useless.

I drop to my knees and gently pull the hair off Aria's cheek. The strands have stuck to her paper-thin skin and peel back a layer when I move them. She screams again, not even able to form the word *stop* because it hurts so bad.

Emmit helps Xyris balance himself with the help of a wall, then hurries over to us. His gaze drifts over the burns. There are so many. Her back, arms, and shins are the worst from how she was hiding in the bathroom, but the rest of her body is burnt, too. Her skin ranges from red to blistered to oozing.

"Shh," Emmit coos, trying to soothe Aria's cries. He takes her palm in his left hand and touches her head with his right. "I know it hurts, but you will be all right. I promise."

Aria's sobs wane to quiet cries as Emmit absorbs her pain. His own pale skin turns red with irritation while his magic burns him from the inside out. Aria's open wounds and blisters melt away before my eyes. In minutes, her burns shift from fourth-degree trauma wounds to first and second. She's still in a considerable amount of pain, but she's no longer screaming.

"Scar, can you help Aria walk?" Emmit grunts as he straightens his spine.

"Of course," she says, rushing to take his place.

"I'll get Xyris," I insist.

Emmit flashes me a look of gratitude, then washes all emotion from his face. I get it; in a world where magic reigns supreme, the slightest sign of weakness can wipe you off the board. Even though it's just the five of us, and not a soul here would defy the circle of trust, the Island is always listening. I don't know who she belongs to now. If it's Belle, and she finds out about Emmit's new weakness, I have no doubt she'll kill him.

"It's eerie down here without the glow bugs," Aria says, huddling close to Scarlett. She's trying to be light-hearted and pretend like she's okay, but her words are clipped.

"Just pretend it's a cloudy night. We're used to those," Scarlett adds, offering her own words of comfort.

Before the Darling came, Neverland was stuck in an eternal twilight, but once she and Peter reconnected, the Island shifted. We saw the sun and the stars for the first time in decades. Most nights, the sky was clear and bright. The dark clouds must have come after we left when the magic began to change.

We follow Emmit deeper into the darkness. It feels like we're in a maze of tunnels beneath the mountain with more caverns the further we go. I survey the path, trying to find landmarks in case we need to run back, but the ground is smooth and the walls are blemish-free. Too perfect to be natural. *Why didn't I know it existed? I thought I knew everything about Neverland...* "What is this place?"

"Caves," Emmit says curtly. He looks over his shoulder and flashes me a look of warning before adding, "Don't tell me you've lost your sense of adventure?"

"Peter?" Xyris says through a forced laugh. "Never."

I mimic the sound but don't comment. I never understood Peter's need to make everyone think he was carefree. The only time he left Neverland was to fetch the Darling and he rarely went beyond his side of the Island. I was the one who went everywhere and saw everything, but no one knows. How could they? The only person who ever heard my voice was Peter.

We walk for what feels like an eternity to the sound of Emmit's humming. I don't recognize the melody, and since no one else has chimed in to sing or hum, too, I'm guessing it's a ballad from his people. There's a lot of unknown about the Fae. I've only ever met the triplets. Everyone else either died or disappeared before I came to be, and it's not like I could ask any questions.

The burden of being a shadow. Always there, but no one minds your existence.

Emmit slows as we approach an opening I recognize. We've reached the Neverpool, a small clearing in the mountain surrounded by stone. It's a little piece of heaven with a peephole view of the sky and a direct connection to the Neversea. Triton created it as a safe space for his land-loving wife to sunbathe without risk of exposure. When she died, he left the magic that keeps it hidden from above in place. We can look up and out into Neverland, but nothing from above the barrier can fall within.

Before us is a glittering night sky and calm seas, but above the night is at war with bursts of red flickering through the overhang of vines. We all step onto the sandy shore of the Neverpool and look up. Scarlett covers her mouth, tears falling down her cheeks as she stares at the fire ravaging our Island. Smoke wraps around the trees as bright red flames swallow them whole. My heart sinks thinking about all the innocent lives being lost. All the creatures who had just come out of their slumber... gone.

"What are we going to do?" Aria asks.

"There's nothing we can do," Emmit says, defeated. "Belle will burn the Island to the ground before losing it."

"I'd say she's definitely losing it," Xyris mumbles. I think it's safe to say we all agree, but no one voices their opinion.

"Scar, help me get Aria into the water." Emmit peels off his shirt. It's sticky with sweat and blood and takes a layer of burned skin with it when he tosses the fabric to the shore. The new wound is bright red and angry, but you'd never know if it hurts. Emmit's face is a mask of indifference, even as he absorbs all of Aria's weight.

"Peter said never to swim in the grotto," Scarlett cautions. She looks at me for guidance, and for a moment, I almost agree.

But then I remember that I am supposed to be Peter and while I agree with the warning, I am trusting that Emmit knows what he's doing. I have no other choice.

"The waters are healing," Emmit says as he and Aria wade waist-deep and then sit. Their heads bob above the surface and he sighs, the tension he held visibly releasing. "Hold your breath," he says to Aria right before pushing her head under.

I count the seconds. *One. Two. Six...* before she finally resurfaces at ten. The red tint to her cheeks is gone. Her honey-colored skin is a crisp golden, as if she's tanned all day, and her fried black hair is wet but lush. They walk out of the grotto's waters, drenched but able to move with ease. Both of them look as good as they had on Neverland's beach the night before Peter and I left. Happy. Healthy. And alive.

"What did that cost?" I ask because nothing comes for free. Magic wants payment for what it gives. Being made from it, I gave freely without repercussion because I could. But for everyone else, it comes with a price.

"Nothing," a cheery voice says from the center of the pool. There's a splash of water and then silence. I wait, too many painful heartbeats to count for the creature to return.

I don't like mermaids. They're unpredictable. I never know if they're going to play with their kill before drowning them or make their suffering seamless with a quick death. Either way, all souls know to stay out of the water because these monsters are just as blood-hungry as Belle.

"But you should find the princess. Time is running out," the creature says.

She uses her arms to crawl onto the water's edge. She lays on her belly and flexes her seafoam green tail until her fins poke up through the murky brown, while long blonde hair falls over her shoulders, concealing her bare breasts. Her skin is the shade of sand with glittering green scales on her forearms that match her tail. I've only seen a mermaid this close once and hoped to never again, but through Peter's eyes, I can understand the desire to draw near. She's one of Neverland's rarest beauties.

And one of its most dangerous creations.

"We have a princess?" Aria asks with childlike wonder. She takes a step toward the water's edge. I grab her wrist and tug her closer to me. Their voices are magic in themselves, designed to lure prey to them. They volley between this world and the connecting realms, feasting on whoever is foolish enough to get close.

The mermaid cocks her head to the side. "Can you not feel her? She's strong but young and in need of guidance." The creature turns her black eyes to me. "He watches over her, but his power is not enough."

"Who is *he?*" Aria asks. Her lack of fear for the creature is concerning. She looks at the beastly like she is a jewel to behold. Not a monster who could rip her throat out.

The creature holds out her hand, her voice a lullaby in the air. "Come. I'll show you."

Aria takes another step toward the seabeast, but I hold her back. "Leave my Lost alone," I demand.

The mermaid frowns at me. "A wolf in sheep's clothing is still a wolf, Dark One. The queen is coming and when she finds you..." The creature's lips pull back into a razor-sharp smile. "I want to be there to see what she does."

"I'm not afraid of Belle." I might be, just a little, but only because an idiot wouldn't fear her. Without my powers, I'm as mortal as the Lost. I may have fed on the souls of the living to keep my strength in the other world, but I meant what I said to Wednesday. I reap death, not succumb to it. If I'm going to die it will be because I chose to sacrifice myself. Not to because I'm some demented fairy's dinner.

"The Fae?" the mermaid scoffs. "She wishes. That one will get what's coming to her, too."

"Who is the queen?" Scarlett asks. She inches forward, but I'm not worried. There are a dozen feet between her and the water's edge. Not to mention Emmit. With as hard as he's fought to keep everyone alive, I doubt he will allow her life to be risked.

The mermaid ignores Scarlett's question and turns her attention to Emmit. "They've tipped the scales of fate and Daddy is not happy. Both must die or everyone will."

He nods. "Understood."

"I could stay," the mermaid holds out her hand again, "If someone wants to play with me. I have so much more to tell."

"You've given us plenty, Serena," Emmit interjects, his voice firm. "Your debt is paid."

The mermaid frowns but pushes herself back into the water. In seconds, she's deep enough to swim away and disappear. The tension in the room snaps, Serena's spell lifting as soon as she's out of sight.

"You know her?" Xyris asks. He's walking better. A little stiff, like he's sat too long, but able to support himself solely and no longer limping. I don't know if the Island has chosen to heal him or if Emmit absorbed enough of his pain too, but I'm glad to see everyone starting to feel like themselves again.

"I was there the day Belle killed Athena." Emmit walks to the water's edge and dips his toes in.

Without the pull of magic, it's just a grotto. A beautiful piece of scenery meant to be enjoyed under the sun, but this land has blood on it. I could feel the heaviness when I was in shadow form and avoided this part of the Island. Like calls to like and it reminded me that I was made from the pieces Peter rejected. The hatred. The obsession. The darkness in him.

Emmit stares out at the vastness of the night. "She would have killed Serena, too, had I not interfered."

Aria gasps and touches her chest. "Why?"

Emmit chuckles darkly. "Why save her or why kill her?"

"Both."

For the first time tonight, he lets raw emotion bleed into his features. Sadness. Pain. And regret. All feelings I've felt too fully since being grounded in this body. "Belle needed the tears of a mermaid to create her time dust and I could only save one."

"Shit." Xyris puts his arm around Emmit and pulls him closer. "That's rough. Sorry you had to go through that, babe."

"That's life with Belle. She doesn't care who gets hurt so long as she wins. Hence the fires." He looks up at the dome above us. The fire rages on, so fiercely there is no darkness. Just the light of death. If not for the magical dome, we'd be dead. "She's trying to flush us out."

"What do we do?" Scarlet looks at me and then so do the others.

One by one, desperate eyes find mine. They're looking at me as their beacon of hope. Like their savior. Like I should be the

King of the Island with a magical shadow that can put an end to everything.

I'm not any of those things.

I swallow hard and try to think of what Peter might say. He always had a way of cheering the others up when they were at their lowest. He understood what true darkness felt like and never wanted anyone else to be where he was.

But I lived in darkness. I relished in the cold and the anger. I fed off the fear and the worry. I used his weaknesses to make myself strong. I made the Island listen to my wishes because it knew all I wanted was to keep it safe. We were on the same page when I was a shadow.

Yet, as a man, it wants nothing to do with me. It's rejected me. After all these years of camaraderie, everything I've ever known has turned upside down. I don't have soothing words. I don't have the fighting skills, that muscle memory as well as every memory Peter formed on these lands has left me. I am like the Lost, hopeless in a new world, wanting nothing more than for my life to be what it once was.

"Peter?" Scarlett asks again. "What do we do?"

Yes, Peter, I think to myself, the Island, and whoever else might be listening. *What do we do?*

CHAPTER 20

James

I laid with Wednesday through most of the night, despite not sleeping. I should have been at the helm guiding us home, but my clock is ticking. I can feel something coming, the dread clings to me like fog on the water, and I can't shake it. All I can do is prepare everyone for what comes next and relish the moments I've been given.

Smee doesn't bother knocking. She never has because there's no point. That woman has seen every inch of my body and helped close wounds in places blood should never seep from. She's been loyal, worthy of my trust, and in turn I've kept nothing from her. But from the way she watches Wednesday, I sense there's something she is keeping from me. "We've crossed into Neverland, Cap, but you're going to want to see this."

I kiss the side of Wednesday's cheek. Her skin is so soft. I could touch her every day and not be satisfied. Returning to the land of the living broke her. Not nearly as much as it had Wendy, but enough. The few updates I could pry out of Peter about my late wife were heartbreaking. Mental institutions and medicine became a factor in Wendy Darling's everyday life after leaving Neverland until she learned to keep her stories to herself. It was only then that she was able to start a new family that she found happiness again. She let us and everything to do with her past go.

Whereas this Darling girl is a fighter. I doubt she'll ever give up on what she believes in, which is why I think the Island chose her. I don't have proof, not yet. But I suspect the changes Neverland is undergoing have everything to do with it crowning a new queen.

The tether that binds us together pulls tighter the further I drift, but something else tugs at my core, too. Grey smoke fills what's left of the night sky. I pull the neck of my shirt over my nose and try to keep from coughing. Black clouds are every-where. They cover the moon in the sky and reach down to the water like the hand of death.

"Where's all this coming from?" I ask.

Smee points to a small flicker of light in the distance. "Never-land's on fire."

"Oh my gods," Wednesday whispers from behind me. I turn and pull her into my side. This isn't the kind of shock she should bear alone. She covers her mouth and stares at the blaring red light that swallows the horizon.

"Your gods can't save you here, Darling," Smee comments. She steps to the guardrail and rests her elbows on the wood. "Can't save them either."

"Smee," I warn. If Belle's pillow talk means anything, the gods of old could be near, and if that's true, the last thing I want is to piss them off. The stars above know we already have our work cut out for us.

"Who could have done this?"

"Who do you think?" Smee chides. Wednesday lets the venom roll off her back, but I'm not having it. I don't believe in punishment by shame. Unless it's a capital offense, all repri-mands are dealt with on an individual basis. I'm going to have to have a word with her about her attitude. Like it or not, so long as I am captain, the Darling is a part of our crew.

"Cass," Wednesday says, and there's a shake to her voice that's troubling.

"The Fae prince?" Smee scoffs. "That boy is as useful as tits on a bull." She turns her ire to me. "This has Belle written all over it. We never should have left the pirates alone with that crazy bitch."

She's right on both accounts, but agreeing with her in front of others would signal that I am unfit to be captain. While my crew is loyal, Smee has made another good point. I have been distracted since Wednesday came aboard. One strike on the leaderboard is fine. Two is treading thin waters. But three—letting anyone know about the poison in my veins or how I haven't healed yet—could lead to mutiny. "It's only been a few hours."

"And look what she's done to our home?" Smee shouts, gesturing to Neverland.

I press my lips together into a fine line. I see the damage and hear the silent screams that echo in the night. I don't need to witness the carnage to know we've lost almost, if not every, soul we saved. Their deaths are infinite. They forfeited their chance at an afterlife when they climbed aboard my ship. Something else I never mentioned because so long as Pan was the Never King no one could die.

"I have to get to the Island," Wednesday says in a panic. She pushes my arm away, takes a few steps, pauses, looks at the fire again—her eyes wide with worry—then turns her attention back to my ship.

"We can't bring the Jolly Roger to port," Smee scolds as if the Darling were a child. "It's not safe."

"I'll find another way." Wednesday spots what she's looking for and runs across the deck to where the rowboat is tied. It hangs off the port side, secured tightly by a pair of pulleys. She tugs at the ropes, hastily trying to get them undone, without a clue as to how the system works.

"Everyone is probably dead by now, Darling. If you go over there you will be, too, but please." Smee folds her arms over her chest and leans against the taffrail. "Keep working those knots."

"You're wrong!" she snaps as tears fall down her cheeks. I've never heard the Darling yell. Even Wendy was cool-tempered. Her cheeks would flush red and her mouth would press together until her lips were barely a thin line, but she never raised her voice. It's startling to hear Wednesday speak with such raw emotion.

But it's not anger that fuels her fire. It's fear for a loved one. The blow of knowing I am one step closer to losing her stings, but I meant what I said. Whoever she chooses, I will support her. Even if she doesn't choose me. "He's fine."

"Who?" Wednesday snaps her gaze up to my face.

"Peter," I say, although by the way her brows push together, I'm not sure that's who she's worried about anymore.

"Peter can take care of himself. I need to get to Cass!" She hastily tugs on the ropes again. If she'd slow down, she'd see the pulleys are engraved with arrows and she is trying to move the wrong rope, but people tend to let fear wipe logic from their minds, and while I don't doubt the Darling could figure out the mechanism under normal circumstances, she is struggling.

"The prince?" Suddenly, it dawns on me that I might already be too late. The other half of her heart, the space I once filled, the only chance I had at winning a place in her life, might already be occupied. "Oh."

"You've got it wrong," Wednesday says hastily, then changes the subject with "And why do you keep calling him a prince?"

"His father was the late Never King," I say reactively. I wait for a flicker of excitement or some kind of acknowledgment that she could be the next princess to register, it would make sense that Neverland wants her as a queen if she is already destined to be royalty, but when her face remains expressionless, I rethink her words and ask," What do yeh mean I've got it wrong."

"I don't care if he lives or dies. I just need what he stole from me." She untwists the wrong rope and the lifeboat starts to slide over the side, without her in it. Panic flashes in her eyes.

I grab the end of the rope and wrap it around my hand. The rope pulls, burning my flesh, but the vessel doesn't crash into the water. "What's worth risking your life for?"

Wednesday chews on her lip. Those tears flood her eyes again. I can see her fighting with them, not sure if she can trust me with her secrets. I understand that war. Some are worth dying for, while others are worth risking. The question is, what kind of secret is this?

A long beat of silence stretches between us. Just when I think Wednesday has given up on me and decided I'm not trustworthy, she looks at me and says, "My daughter."

CHAPTER 21
Wednesday

Everything smells like death.

Ash floats in the air, mixing with smoke. It's impossible to breathe without a bandanna over my face, let alone see more than a few feet in front of us. The deep blue water fades to an ugly gray the closer we get to shore, but thankfully nothing dead floats on its surface. It might not count for much considering how many lives have been lost on the Island, but I am glad the sea seems to have been spared.

James rows us to shore. My gaze darts from the sky-high flames and his flexing muscles. I try not to look at either option, but I can't help myself. One sight has me anxious with anticipation. The other... well, James makes me anxious for many reasons. He's barely said anything to me since I mentioned Mira. Beyond offering to help me get to the sand and asking if I was ready, James has been painfully quiet.

I don't know why, but his silence hurts.

Despite the awkward tension and a weird desire to climb onto James's lap every five minutes, I'm grateful he's here. Sexy sailor needs aside, I'm not sure I would have been able to navigate from the ship to the Island on my own. The Neversea fights him with every row, using its waves to try and push us back out into the ocean, but James is strong and takes us to the only spot on the Island that hasn't caught fire—a plot of land just south of Peter's treehouses.

The sun peeks over the horizon as James climbs out of the rowboat and jumps into knee-deep water. He grips the wood siding and pulls me to shore. As soon as the bow meets the sand,

I hop out so he can drag the boat up the bank and away from the ocean.

James wipes the sweat from his brow with the back of his arm. His gaze bounces from the rowboat to the water a few times before finding peace with his thoughts. "If the tide shifts, it should be safe."

He analyzes the boat and situates the oars and ropes while I face the Neverforest. From the *Jolly Roger*, this section of the woods looked small. I thought it might be a few dozen feet in each direction, but now that I see it up close, it doesn't look so manageable. The dense greenery is vast. I can't even see the glow of the fire. It's like there's a magical barrier protecting this section of the Island.

My toes sink into the sand as I walk toward the furthest edge. I think I know why this land hasn't been swallowed by the fire yet, but I need proof. Something solid to go on because a theory won't bring me closer to Mira.

I walk along the water's edge and recognize the picnic table we used to party at—tiny gray flakes cover it like a blanket. I try not to think about the last time I sat there or everything that came after. If I do, doubt will creep in and I refuse to believe all of this is anything but reality. My daughter is real and that wall of fire ten yards away is also very real.

I stop walking and let my brain catch up to my racing heart. Logically, there should be a line of forever frost on the ground. Or maybe a blanket of it on the other side of the trees. Perhaps an ice wall? No... I would see the ice shimmering in the sun, there's something here. Some form of Cass's magic and I'm determined to find out what it is.

The fire may not be moving, but whatever the magic is that's holding them back doesn't work on the heat. Waves of hot air stick to my skin and lungs and I'm still twenty feet from the fire line. My arms feel like I have a sunburn, only I haven't been in the sun. They hurt even though they aren't red.

"I don't think so." James grabs me by the shirt collar and

pulls me back a few feet. The temperature difference in the air is staggering.

"Let me go!" I twist free of his hold and glare. "I wasn't going to walk into the fire. I just wanted to see the edge and find out why it hasn't crossed over."

"That's not happening," he scoffs. "Fire isn't the only thing that kills, Sunshine, and yeh are too important to risk. Magic holds the flames back. Don't try to understand it. Just accept it."

"I have to know why the fire isn't moving!" I shout, feeling every bit like a child having a tantrum, but he doesn't understand. There's a need too strong. I feel like I might explode if I don't discover whose magic is saving Neverland. In my mind, it can only be Cass keeping the Island safe. I *need* it to be Cass because that means Mira is safe. If someone else saved Neverland but didn't save my daughter, my heart would break.

"Yehr letting fear shift yehr focus, Sunshine. Yehr not here to save the Island. Yehr here to save yehr daughter while yeh still can." James grabs my shoulders and looks me in the eyes. His determination tickles at a memory, but I can't find which one. I try to search the archives of my mind, but everything is gone. I can't access Wendy's past now that I'm back in Neverland.

"Don't lose yehr daughter like I lost my boys, Wednesday." He swallows hard and takes a minute to say, "Yeh'll hate yehself if yeh do."

James never says my name. I've been Sunshine since the moment we met. Hearing him call me anything else is like a crack of thunder on a summer's day. Loud. Purposeful. And out of place.

"You're right," I admit. I push my hair back with one hand, gather it in my palm, then let it go. Shit. I thought losing my cat was heartbreaking. I thought it helped me understand the suffering Peter went through when he lost his nephews, but an animal isn't the same as a child. And a secondhand loss, while horrible, doesn't come close to losing your child. James lost two. "Help me. Please."

"Close yehr eyes, love." James waits patiently for me to find my bearings again. It's hard to choke back the constant worry and need to cry, but I can't be weak forever. Mira needs me, and I am too close to fuck this up.

I close my eyes and James says, "Yehr her mother. The magic tying yeh to yehr daughter is in yehr veins. All yeh need to do is tap into it. Reach for her. Call out to her. Find the thread of life that binds yeh and pull it tight. Make the Island tell yeh where she is. It will do what yeh say. All yeh have to do is ask."

Ask.

Ask the Island to tell me where my daughter is. Yeah. Okay.

I feel silly, but I use my thoughts to call out for Mira. *Where are you, sweet girl?*

In the real world, all this talk of magic would be crazy, but this is Neverland. Anything is possible. I traveled on a flying ship. I've dined with people whose lives were lost before I was even born. I've crossed through space and time, somehow skipping three years of my life. I lived on an island that should only exist in storybooks. I've fucked and fell in love with the man, the Shadow, and have very strong feelings for his brother. None of it should be possible, but here I am. Living proof that if you believe in magic the world is at your fingertips.

I choose to believe Neverland listened to my pleas and brought me home. Just like I choose to believe it will lead me to my daughter.

The invisible string James mentioned pulls tight in my chest. It guides me, physically moving my shoulders and twisting me to my right. I imagine myself yanking on the rope and whatever is on the other side fights back. I snap my eyes open and point. "There."

"Good. She listens to yeh."

"Who?" I open my eyes. "Mira?"

James grins and I see a flicker of resemblance between him and Peter. The mischief. The madness. Perhaps even a little magic. "No, Neverland."

"That's absurd." I laugh. Neverland belongs to Peter Pan. If it listens to me, it's because I am tied to him. The other half of his soul it feels obligated to entertain.

"Prove me wrong," he says with a challenge. "Ask the Island to bring yeh something. If it does, we have our answer. It helps many but only serves one."

And what should I ask for? Breakfast? I roll my eyes. Even though I am hungry and would love a mango or some toast and cloudberry lemonade, this distraction is exactly what James said we should be avoiding. "We don't have time for this. After we find my daughter, I'll play your game, but we need to go."

I take off into the woods, following the pull of the thread that binds us. With every step, it pulls tighter. I'm a fish on a string. A yoyo to its master. I can physically feel her calling to me.

And I'll do whatever it takes to get to her.

Chapter 22

Wednesday

It's funny how different a memory can feel when you're staring at its origin.

I often dreamed of the Lost's treehouses. Each built from wood harvested from the Neverforest or found on the Island's shore. At least ten feet off the ground, they are connected by wooden rope bridges, with Peter's being at the center of it all like a spider with its web. Heidi's house was the closest, a mere twenty feet from the web's center, with the others spreading out to offer privacy.

Cass's treehouse is smaller than the rest. He only had the one bedroom. All the others had at least two. Emmit's even had three, although I'm not sure why. It's not like he could have kids and up until recently, the Island only seemed to welcome adults.

Cass's treehouse is also furthest from the rest. It's bridge to the group's center feels miles long. I never cared enough to count my steps or to wonder why he'd want to be so far from his friends, but now I'm curious if the distance is intentional. If he always planned to betray Peter, or if his plan came to fruition after I arrived.

The last time I was on the Island, he said he'd been trying to reclaim his home for centuries. Hundreds of human years of failed efforts, with the last hundred—give or take—having Peter thrown into the mix. I can't imagine knocking up a mortal was where he saw his life going. Then again, I can't imagine him doing all the other terrible things he's done. Had I not been the victim or seen it with my own eyes, I wouldn't have believed it.

"Yeh alright there, Sunshine?" James looks at me and I swear all I've seen in his eyes since stepping foot back on this Island is worry. I'm sure the pain he feels is because of what happened to the pirates. He lost one family to Neverland and now it's claimed another. I just happen to be his current focus so he doesn't break down.

"Yup," I lie because I most definitely am not. I'm guessing this is what those *Law and Order* victims feel like when they confront their attackers. I always felt bad for them, but excited at the same time as I watched the characters finally get their justice. But I'm not looking for justice. I'm looking for Mira and I'm a bundle of nerves out of fear that she might not be here.

"What's yehr plan?" James asks.

That is a great question. I never thought I'd get this far. My plan stopped at getting to Neverland because that felt next to impossible. "Don't have one. Figured I'd knock on the door and play the surprise card. Worked well enough for him."

"He won't hurt yeh," he says, seeing through the mask of bravery I'm trying to wear.

I raise my eyebrows and force a laugh. "You clearly don't know him well. Cass is a psychopath."

"Must be a familial trait." James rubs the scruff on his cheek. "But the prince *can't* hurt yeh. If what I think is happening is happening, then he's in for a world of shit."

"Did coming back to the Island tie your tongue or something? Because you're starting to sound like Cass."

"Gods, I hope not." James laughs and despite the severity of where we stand, it sounds genuine. "Just trust yehrself. No thought is too crazy, no wish is too far-fetched. Yeh want him dead...then strike him down. Yeh want him to suffer...imagine him in pain. Or if yeh just want to grab yehr daughter and go we can do that, too. Whatever yeh choose, I'm here if yeh need me. No questions asked. I've got yehr back."

"Thank you, James." I touch his arm and a sizzle of heat passes between us. "I'm really glad you're here."

I step in front of the rope ladder that leads to Cass's porch and stare up at the path I need to climb. The last time I was here, a small part of me locked up every time I had to work my way up or down a ladder, but this time, I'm not afraid. Falling to the ground feels trivial compared to everything I've been through.

So, what if it hurts? Who cares if I break a bone? Life hurts. Living has been the most difficult and painful experience, but it's had some great moments, too. I never thought I'd become best friends with my sister. I never imagined the warmth and joy growing a child would give me. I didn't expect the pain of losing a lover to amplify the excitement of finally finding another. I've traveled the world and done things I never thought possible.

This stupid ladder is nothing.

I grab the first peg and pull myself up. Eighteen steps are all that separate me from Mira. Eighteen notches, each about a foot apart, and then I'll finally have my baby girl in my arms again. I climb, reaching one arm up to the next peg before moving my foot. It's easy enough, but I don't rush the process. I take my time, going what probably feels snail-slow to James, but he doesn't say anything. He climbs beneath me, patiently waiting for me to make my next move.

The middle peg about halfway up is slick. My foot slips, throwing me off balance and the bravery I felt is gone. In a split second that fear of falling and the anticipation of pain floods my senses. James grabs my waist the moment my balance wavers and steadies me. "Easy, Sunshine. I don't think yehr ready to fly yet."

I force a laugh, feeling my heartbeat everywhere, and light-heartedly say, "That'll be the day."

James holds me tight while I get my bearings again. I don't take long, just a minute at most, then keep making my way up to Cass's platform. I peek my head through the panel cut into the patio floor, searching for any sign that he saw us coming. Seconds tick by without movement. When I feel confident it's safe, I finish climbing the last steps and then hoist myself back onto solid ground.

James pops up like a daisy, effortlessly finding his feet again and taking his stance just outside of the front door's view. He draws his sword, holding it in his right hand, ready to fight. "Are yeh ready?"

"Is that necessary?" I ask, eyeing the two-and-a-half-foot piece of metal.

"Hopefully not, but yeh never can be sure which is why it's made from iron, not steel. Metal will cut a Fae, but it won't slow them down. They'll be bloody and pissed off, but still standing whereas iron will incapacitate them. It's one of the few weaknesses these creatures have."

"Good to know. What's another?" I'm stalling. I don't know why. I should be knocking and preparing to face off with Cass, ready to go full mamma bear on him. Instead, I'm wasting precious minutes, trying to muster up the courage to see him again while hoping I don't puke all over myself.

James reaches in front of me and pounds on the door. He gives me a silent nod, then steps back into the shadows and out of sight. He knew I needed a push, just like he knew I needed saving. I smile at him, yet again grateful for his presence. I almost wish it was him I had met at the bar, and not Peter, all those moons ago. But the thought feels wrong as soon as it crosses my mind. I may not understand or fully like the path I was thrown on, but it is mine. For better or for worse, this is where I'm meant to be.

"I swear to the stars, Belle," Cass's voice carries from deep inside his treehouse. "If you hurt a single hair on her head, I'll—"

The door whips open and Cass's words die. He stares at me, eyes wide, all the color draining from his face. A nervous smile tugs at my lips, but I hold it back by pressing them tight together. My feeble heart races at his beauty, but my mind reminds me that he is deadly.

And apparently, an idiot who can't keep track of the most important thing in both of our lives.

I place my hands on my hips and level my stare with his ice-blue eyes. "Whose hair are you worried about, Cass? Because I swear to every star in the sky, if you lost our daughter, I'll kill you."

CHAPTER 23
Wednesday

"Thank the stars." Cass grabs me by the wrist and pulls me inside. He slams the door shut and then wraps me in a hug. I lock up for a moment as he buries his face in my shoulder, holding me like I'm his long-lost lover and not the girl he knocked up and tried to kill. "I never thought I'd be happy to see you again, but damn it, Darling, you're a sight for sore eyes."

Anger simmers under my skin. How dare he use me to soothe his agony when all he's done is cause mine. I press my palms to Cass's chest to shove him away, but the narcissistic prick is immovable, probably under the delusion that I'm here because I forgive him. I arch my back and push harder, barely able to make an inch between our bodies. "Get off of me, asshole."

No sooner than the words leave my lips does the front door swing open and clamor against the wall. Cass moves with a speed that can only be explained as Fae because, in less than a second, I am tucked safely behind him, his right hand is spread wide while a small flurry of snow plays in his palm.

James steps into the open space, his sword drawn and pointed at Cass's face. The sight is breathtaking. Every fantasy I had as a girl about Orlando Bloom has flooded my brain again. I swallow hard and try not to stare at the corded muscles of his arm or think about how this man is every bit of the fairytale prince I always dreamed of. Wendy's novel about Peter Pan painted James as the villain, and maybe, in some ways, he was in her story, but in mine he's the unexpected hero. The love interest that snuck up on me. The man I almost wish I had met first.

"Yeh heard the girl." James tips his wrist and motions for Cass to move.

"Interesting." Cass takes a large step to my left. His hand relaxes and the tiny storm in his palm dissipates. His gaze bounces from James to me, twice, then settles on the purple marks peeking out beyond the collar of James's shirt. "Very interesting."

I swallow the heady desire I seem to fight whenever James is near and turn my focus to the treehouse. The living room is the same, the wall shelves are still filled with too many trinkets to count, and he's still got the same tattered oversized chairs and driftwood-carved end table. At quick glance, there isn't a single hint in the main space to indicate that Mira is here, but I know she is.

I can feel it.

The anticipation of finally reuniting with my daughter twists my stomach into knots. I'm nervous. Excited. And terrified. I don't know how to be a mother. I read all of Tyle's old *What to Expect* books because she swore they prepared her for all the ups and downs of her pregnancy. I found them boring and hardly helpful, which is why I never graduated to the next stage of the series. And after Mira was taken, I didn't see the point. Not until I had her in my arms again. Now I wish I had read them because that moment is here and I am low-key freaking out.

"Mira?" I call out while walking toward Cass's bedroom.

Less than twenty paces and I'm through the hallway and into his tiny space. It was always the barest room out of all the tree-houses, having only a bed and minimal necessities, but it's fuller now. There is a small cradle carved from wood with a rocking base near the far wall and some odd-looking bottles on the bedside table. Cloth squares are laid out on the dresser top that I think might be diapers and he's hung some dried branches with woven flowers from the ceiling above the cradle. Little by little, I find clues that confirm this is where Cass brought Mira.

But she's not here.

I search every inch of the room, just in case he's hidden her somewhere. Under the bed. In the bathroom. Beneath the pile of dirty clothes in the corner, not likely, but I can't leave a single inch untouched. I refuse to believe that she's gone and that Cass is stupid enough to have lost our daughter. I make my way to the kitchen and open every cabinet just in case Cass hid her somewhere in there on the off chance that he could sense my arrival. I empty everything, throwing it all behind me until each shelf is bare.

Pressure builds in my chest as I sit on the kitchen floor, surrounded by everything Cass owns, and my heart races. Something wraps itself around my lungs until I can't draw in a clean breath. The air physically hurts my chest and my skin feels like someone is poking it with a thousand needles.

I traveled the world, literally crossed the universe to find my daughter, and she's not here.

The room spins around me. Everything swirls and tilts to one side like it does when I'm on a carnival ride. My hands sweat as a cold blanket of air washes the color from my face. Saliva floods my mouth, warning me that if I don't get my shit together soon, I'm going to puke. I try and swallow it but there's too much. I spit it on the floor and then wipe away the mess with a dish towel.

Cass reaches for my arm. He looks genuinely concerned, which is surprising. I didn't think he could care for anyone but himself. "Darling?"

"Don't touch her," James snaps. He steps behind me and pulls me to my feet. My cold body presses against his warm chest. The heat is a shock to my system, but in a good way. I feel the rise and fall of his steady breaths and try to keep my own breathing in sync with his. The weight of his arms around my belly is steadying. Everything begins to find its place again and, although I could use a glass of water, I feel a little better.

Cass tries to come close again, but James effortlessly raises his sword. "I would think twice if yeh value yehr life, mate."

"You can't kill me," Cass chides incredulously. The snarl he gives is feral, like a cat caged, ready to attack. I doubt the reaction has anything to do with me, but it's obvious he feels threatened.

"Maybe not," James quips. "But she can."

"Impossible." Cass's gaze bounces to me again. He studies my face as if it's the first time we've met, almost like he believes James. There's a hatred in his eyes, but curiosity, too.

James lowers his sword and chooses to stand beside me rather than behind me. His stance is relaxed, but his grip on the handle of his weapon is tight. "Enlighten me, Prince, did stealing the child give yeh the power yeh craved?"

"Power?" I look over to James. "What are you talking about?"

"Tell her," James insists, never breaking his focus on Cass to look at me.

Cass exhales heavily and runs his hands through his hair. He steps around the mess on the floor and finds a green bottle I set beside a pile of cups. "I need a drink for this. Wine?"

He's joking. He has to be.

But as an extra second ticks by with Cass doing nothing but staring at me, I realize he's not. "As if I'd trust anything from you again."

"Fair point." Cass pops the cork and pours himself a glass. I recognize the scent, but can't pinpoint what flavor they might be. I tried so many the last time I was here. He swallows the first round like a shot, then adds, "Sorry about that."

"Him?" James asks, reading between the lines. I planned to keep the details of who tried to kill me to myself, but with Cass's admission, there is no point in lying. I nod and a deep growl vibrates in James's chest.

"What? I said I was sorry." Cass's ignorance of how much he

hurt me, Peter, Pan, and apparently James is mind-blowing. But what's done is done. I am alive, no thanks to him, and even though I will never forgive Cass, I'm ready to move past it all.

"Why did you take Mira, Cass? And where is she?"

He foregoes the glass and takes his next swallow directly from the bottle. "Years ago, Neverland was a magical hotspot. It was an island built by the gods but given to the Fae. My father ruled alongside Triton and Poseidon and frequently counseled Zeus. You wouldn't believe what it was like growing up here."

"I don't care. Get to the part about Mira."

James sheaths his sword and pulls me into his arms again. They wrap around my waist and I lean against him, our bodies molding together like they were created for each other. "Patience, Sunshine."

Cass rounds the kitchen island and makes himself comfortable in one of the oversized chairs. "The Island itself embodies the magic of the gods. It lives and breathes through its king, the magic tied to his life. When an heir is born, the power shifts to the child but the parents can siphon the wee one's abilities to keep the Island from falling into chaos until their eighteenth birthday."

"So, you were hoping to what... boost your powers through Mira?" I swear, if he thought he could draw from her life to better his, I'll put one of James's iron daggers through his heart. Magic takes from the one who uses it, that's why when Peter and his shadow reunited it almost killed him.

"Neverland was always supposed to be mine!" Cass roars. He clenches his teeth and then forces a smile before taking another sip of his wine. "Emmit had no interest in ruling, and Belle is a girl. She couldn't be king. That left me to take over my father's kingdom, and I was ready!"

"But Neverland chose someone else," James interjects. "Peter."

"Belle lost her mind when the Island denied all three of us. She challenged our father and said we lost our birthright because he was unworthy. Back then, she could command the skies. She channeled the power of Zeus and struck down half our kingdom with his thunderbolts. Father ripped her wings from her back, severing her ties to the Island and all its magic as punishment."

Neither he nor Emmit can fly. Or if they can, I've never seen it. Just like I've never seen a mark on Cass's sculpted back to indicate where his wings could have been. Although, to be fair, I wasn't looking for one the last time he took his shirt off around me. "Is that what happened to your wings?"

Cass shakes his head. "Only the female Fae are born with wings. The bigger and prettier they are, the more powerful children they can bear."

So, she's a peacock. A smile turns my lips until I realize that by losing her wings, not only did Belle lose her ties to the Island, but she may have lost the ability to have children, too. For her, stealing Mira could have a deeper purpose than it does for Cass. "But she has magic still. How?"

"Blood magic," James interjects. "The kind that sends yeh into the darkest pits of Hades hell. Yeh wanted to kill her. Didn't yeh? That's why yeh took the child."

Cass nods once.

There were more years where I hated Tyle than I loved her, but I never wanted anything bad to happen to her. No matter how much hell she put me through, she was my sister. My twin. A bond that Cass should understand since he is a triplet. "But she's your sister!"

"That creature isn't my sister! Tinkerbelle was kind. She loved Neverland. I understand being scared of change, but the shit she's done is unforgivable. Her death and Mira's reign are the only way to make this island what it was. I thought killing Peter would force the Island to choose a new leader. I thought draining him of his powers would prove him unworthy. I thought I would be the next Neverking!" He throws the glass bottle across the room. It hits the wall and shatters. What was left of the wine drips down the wall like blood.

"Where is Mira?" I ask as calmly as possible.

"Belle took her. I went out to create a barrier to keep us safe from the fire. When I came back, she was gone." He pulls open a drawer and hands me a slip of paper. "This was in her crib."

"First of all, it sucks, doesn't it? Losing your child." I grab the note from his hands. "And secondly, who leaves a baby alone? Parenting rule number one is don't forget your child!"

"You left her, too! Remember?"

"Yeah, to walk down the hall. Not alone in a house while I was out in the woods." I swear, this man will be the death of me. I fold the parchment and read the blue swirly letters.

You or her. Make your choice.

"What's that supposed to mean?" I set the note on the countertop and move out of James's arms. I'm hot, and his extra body heat isn't making me feel good. Sweat drips down my back and off my brow. Cass notices and shoots a rush of cool air in my direction. I don't understand him. One minute, he wants to be the bad guy; the next, he's trying to help.

"Belle thinks that if I die, Mira's guardianship will transfer to her. Giving her all of my powers and access to Mira's, too."

"But you don't have any extra powers," I say in a panic.

"I know."

"And there's no guarantee she won't hurt her either way." I run my fingers through my hair and pace the room. This is bad. So very bad.

And it pisses me off that all Cass has to say about the situation is, "I know."

"And if you're dead, there would be no one who can keep Mira safe."

"I know!" Cass yells, slumping into the oversized chair by the window again. "This is fucked. Everything is fucked. I thought I wouldn't care about the kid since bringing Mira to Neverland was pointless, but I can't let her go either. What the hell is wrong with me?"

"It's called fatherhood," James says sympathetically. "It's a blessing and a curse. Yehr happiness is directly tied to yehr kin."

Cass's face hardens. Regret or maybe sorrow flashes in his eyes. "I forgot you had kids."

"How long has Mira been gone?" I ask. Talking about the past won't help. Not in this situation. I feel for James, I do, but we need to stay focused.

"I don't know. A few hours at most. I searched the forest for a sign of how Belle got through the fire. Not long after I got back, you showed up."

I chew on my bottom lip. Why would the Island pull me here if this isn't where Mira was? What was the point?

Clearly, Cass is useless. He would have gone after Belle already if he could have. "What are we going to do?" I mean to ask myself, but the words fall off my lips like a plea to the stars.

"There's not much we can do until the fires die down. The only way to Belle's castle is to take a boat, but without the ability to fly we'd be trapped."

"There are tunnels that run under the mountain. We could steal Mira and escape through them," James suggests.

Cass shakes his head. "It's a maze down there. I know a few of the paths, but one wrong turn and we'd be lost."

"This is bullshit!" I shout. Everything about this is wrong. Peter wouldn't sit around and let the fires take over the Island. Pan wouldn't give up without a fight. We can't either.

"Why does Belle get to burn the place down? Why aren't the fires coming after her, too?"

Cass shrugs. "It's her island."

"No, it's not!" I yell. "She doesn't have the right to kill everything that lives here because she's what... throwing a tantrum!" I open the door and storm outside.

"Where are yeh going?" James yells, chasing after me as I scurry down the ladder.

"To find my daughter."

"You're not strong enough to save her!" Cass yells. "The fires—"

"Screw the fires!"

"Wednesday!" James yells and hearing him use my name again gives me pause. I turn to face him and something falls on my cheek.

I reach up to the wet spot and wipe it away. I rub my fingers together and another drop falls, hitting my arm.

Thunder booms overhead and then the sky opens up. Water pours from the clouds in big, monsoon-like drops. I run back to the overhang and stand under the shelter of Cass's platform.

"It's raining." I watch steam rise from the yielding flames and hope blooms in my chest. If this keeps up, the fires will be out within the hour. Neverland will have a chance to breathe and we can hike towards Belle's castle in the mountain. "It never rains in Neverland."

"Do yeh believe me now?" James wraps his arm around my waist.

I lean into him, oddly relaxed despite the hot air forming around us. "About what?"

"The Island. It listens to yeh. Yeh want the fires put out, it's doing it for yeh."

"Impossible." Cass slides down the ladder. "She only listens to Peter's shadow."

"Yeh said it yehrself, a true heir was born. That child kicked Peter off his throne and made way for a new liege."

"She's human," Cass says, shocked and angry. "She can't be the new ruler."

James steps into the rain and bows, as if that is all the proof he needs. "I humbly pledge my allegiance to yeh, Sunshine. The new Queen of Neverland."

CHAPTER 24

Xyris, stay here with the girls," Emmit directs. "You know where the food and water are. Watch the sky. If we aren't back in two days, take the rowboat to the Jolly Roger. James will give you sanctuary, but move in the night. Belle's guards are mindless, but if she's given the order to execute trespassers, they will without question."

Xyris nods and leans forward to kiss Emmit. The embrace is quick, but I think it's safe to say we all feel the heaviness of this goodbye. The goal is to keep the Lost safe. The endgame, eliminate Belle and take back our Island. The plan...

I'm hoping Emmit has one because I don't.

"What happens in two days?" Scarlett asks. I'm wondering the same thing. It's a very specific amount of time, which leads me to believe Emmit knows more than he's letting on.

"Just stay together and you'll be safe." He dodges the question and takes off into the tunnels again.

Scarlett looks to me for guidance since Emmit hasn't offered any. "Everything will be okay. Xyris will take care of you both until we get back."

If we come back.

I sprint into the darkness to catch up to Emmit. The black blanket around us is smothering. I'm not usually afraid of the dark. I lived in it for so many years that it became a part of me. I could sense the movements of the land and see tiny shifts in the air.

But in Peter's body, my senses are dulled. I have fear and worry for the first time. Worry about tripping. Worry about bleeding, wondering what that pain feels like. I'm so pathetically fragile now. I don't know how much use I'll be in this war.

Perhaps all I am is a decoy. Belle doesn't know Peter is dead or that I exist. That bit of knowledge is the only leverage we have. I just hope Emmit knows how to use it.

I bump into a hard body deep within the maze of tunnels. I swing on instinct and hit the air. The person shuffles back a step and then sighs disapprovingly. "Whatever you're going through, you need to get over it. I need the Neverland Shadow, not this pathetic version of Peter."

Believe me, I'd love to be that man again, too. Given time, I could be, but time isn't a luxury I have. I've been thrown into a magicless body and my only interaction with it in this world was bound by chains. I'm learning and trying my best to adapt, knowing that if I don't Wednesday will think I abandoned her, but it hasn't been easy. "I'm fine. Let's keep going."

I step to the side to go around Emmit. He grabs me by the back of my shirt. "I can smell your fear. You reek of it. What's going on?"

It crosses my mind to lie, to preserve what little dignity I have left, but like me, Emmit is one of the Lost. We are brothers. Bound together in this life by a pact made in blood. Who else is there if I can't trust him with my truths? "I'm not connected to the Island anymore. She's stripped me of all my magic, and I don't know how to be human."

"That's...really fucking shitty." He lets me go. "But you have Peter's memories. He learned to exist without magic. Use them."

"I can't reach them. Something is blocking me from him and them."

"Great. You're basically an oversized toddler. Cute but useless." He's quiet, probably trying to decide if I should be left with the Lost. I'd be less of a hindrance there, but I want to help. "We need to convince Belle that you're Peter. You did a good job of that back at the castle."

"That was before I knew my magic was gone."

"Magic doesn't make the man, Pan. You want to be a coward? Fine. Go back to the grotto and wait for me to return. I don't need a liability. I need a soldier. Someone who will go into battle with me and take back our home."

Every one of the Lost has gone through this moment. That's why Peter named them Lost. The souls come to the Island and don't know up from down anymore. Change will throw you for a loop like that. You can either spin out and lose all control of what's left of your life, or you can take the reins and make the best of where you've landed.

As a shadow, I never understood why the souls on Neverland were tortured. I thought they were pathetic and weak, but I understand now. Without my magic, it feels like I've lost myself. I have no purpose anymore. The island has rejected me, and I'm left to simply exist. It's a hard pill to swallow.

I imagine this is how the souls feel when they arrive. The world they knew is gone. Their families gone. That force that drove them to work and forge a life doesn't exist in Neverland. They have to learn to cope with their losses and adapt to a new way of living. They have all of eternity.

I have mere hours to get myself together.

"I need to get back to Wednesday," is all I offer because it is the only option.

"The only way that will happen is if we kill Belle. Now, let's go."

We walk and walk, turning down unmarked corridors, going gods know where. I stay close, careful not to lose sight of Emmit. The last thing I want is to be lost in this body, wondering these tunnels until I starve to death.

After what feels like an eternity, light filters into the darkness ahead of us. We've found an opening to the outside world, but we could be anywhere on the island. The Never Mountain is at Neverland's heart, split between Peter's half of the Island and James's, but neither of them goes to the east corner, where the late king's castle was carved into the stone. The land over there is in ruins from a battle that happened long before our time. Walking onto it emits a wave of fear that snakes its way into your veins. The magic warding it doesn't want visitors and so we've stayed away. Until today.

"She's here. The Island wants us to find her." He looks at me with hopeful eyes. "Can you feel the pull?"

"Who?" I stand beside Emmit and look out at the rain. I don't feel anything except the heat in the air.

"The new queen."

"Your mermaid friend mentioned her, but who is it?"

"I thought you were smarter than this." Emmit shakes his head. "It feels like she's on the west end of the Island. If we hurry, we can cross paths before they make it to Belle's castle. She's going to need all the help she can get."

I grab his arm as he starts to walk away. I'm tired of the half-truths. I know it's how he was trained to talk, but I'm grasping at straws, trying to keep my head above water. I need a solid answer. "I'm going to need you to slow down a beat, Emmit. I can't feel the Island anymore. Remember? Who are we trying to find?"

He huffs out an impatient breath and says, "Your precious Darling. Wednesday."

CHAPTER 25
Wednesday

"What's the plan?" Cass shouts as we run through the woods. His ignorance to us trying to be stealthy is frustrating. We're already loud enough, unable to control the sound of half-burnt branches snapping beneath our feet and Cass was zero help in telling us what Belle's guard is like. We don't know how far from the side of the mountain they stretch or what their orders are if they discover intruders.

The likely answer? Capture or kill. Both of which we cannot let happen.

"I don't have one."

"Of course you don't," he mutters.

I stop running and brace my hands on my knees. My lungs burn. Legs hurt. I forgot that everywhere we go in Neverland is on foot. After catching my breath, I stand upright but keep my hands over my head for another minute. "Improvising worked well with you. Maybe Belle will hug me, too."

"Unlikely," Cass scoffs. His patience grows thinner the longer we're together. I can't read him. One minute, the man is hot; the next, he's cold.

"Watch yehr tone," James warns. "But Cass is right. We can't go to the castle half-cocked. If she throws her dust, we're done for. It's been three days since she last fed. She'll be weaker but still deadly."

"How do you know?" Cass asks.

James pulls the corner of his shirt to show the stitches on his shoulder and the purple veins that stretch from the mark.

"There were no new souls in the Neversea. I offered one of my memories to keep the Pirates from having to sacrifice again."

"She did this to you?" The marks look horrible. I knew they looked wrong, but I never would have imagined they were from a bite wound. I trace over one of the purple lines with my finger. The skin is raised, similar to a burn scar. Textured, yet soft.

"You should be dead," Cass says with zero emotion.

James adjusts his shirt to cover as many of the marks as possible, but they peek out over his shirt collar. There's no hiding how she's hurt him. "It's a miracle I'm not."

The sound of snapping branches and rustling of leaves has us all turning our heads. James pulls his sword from his holster and steps in front of me. Cass flicks his wrists and a glowing blue ball appears in his palms. Both men are ready for battle and I...

I don't even have a weapon to defend myself with.

"Show yourself!" Cass demands.

"Always with the orders," someone shouts, and I recognize the voice. Emmit pushes aside a half-charred palm frond and steps into view. "Hello, brother."

"Emmit!" I run forward and throw my arms around his neck. I'm so relieved he's okay and hopeful for the others. I tried not to think about what might have happened to them in the fires. The way the flames swallowed everything in their path, I hoped the Lost made it out alright. Any other outcome was unacceptable, but there haven't been any signs of life. Everything we pass is either black or ashen and the whole island smells like death.

"It's good to see you, too, Your Majesty." He steps out of our embrace and bows. "I have a gift for you."

My cheeks flush pink and I stifle a laugh. I am the furthest thing from a queen and for some reason, even Emmit thinks I'm one. Cass rolls his eyes and puts out the snow flurry in his palm. I scowl at him as someone else steps through the clearing. I recognize the silhouette, but don't let myself get excited until I see his face.

"Peter!" I leap forward into his arms. "I was so scared something had happened to you."

Peter barely touches me. His body is like a wall, hard and cold, and his voice... It's broken. "Something did."

I look into dark eyes and gasp. "Pan?" I whisper. "But how?"

He sets me on my feet and tucks his hands in his pockets. "I don't know, but Peter's gone. So are my ties to Neverland."

I cup his cheeks and look into his eyes. This isn't the broody spirit I love. This man is broken, and it breaks my heart to see him this way. I want to pull him into my arms and reassure him that everything will be all right, but he steps back, putting inches that feel like miles between us. "Are you okay?"

He shrugs sadly. "I'll survive. That's what you mortals do. Right?"

James places his hand on my belly and pulls me back a step while he comes forward and draws his sword at Pan. "Stay away from our queen."

Pan holds his hands up. "It's bad form to challenge an unarmed opponent."

"Stop this!" I push James's sword down and the Island rumbles. "No fighting. Pan is my friend, not my enemy. I know you've had your differences in the past, but if you can't put them aside and work together, then I don't want you here. Understand?"

"Yes, my lady," James agrees begrudgingly. He sheaths his sword but doesn't move from my side.

I turn to Pan. "And you? Can I trust you to have my back with both Cass and James there, too?"

"Doesn't seem like I have a choice. I'm not leaving you." There's the fire in his eyes I was looking for. A small glimpse that the man I know is buried somewhere deep inside.

"Good." I reach for his hand and squeeze it. "Because I think I might have a plan, but it's going to take all of us to make it work."

"And what is it? Because five minutes ago, you were drawing a blank," Cass sneers.

I look at him and wonder which man is the real one. This arrogant jerk or the one who took me into the Never Caves to see their version of stars. I will never forgive Cass for all the pain he's put me through, but that doesn't mean I don't miss who he used to be when we were together. "Do you remember what you told me never to say?"

"No," he says flatly.

"Go on," Emmit encourages. I see the gears turning in his head, and I think he might be on the same page as me.

"Well, what if we get me in the room with Belle and I say it?"

Emmit paces back and forth. He knows the Fae laws better than I do. I hope he's deciding if my plan is doable because it's the only one I've got. Finally, he stops walking to meet my gaze. "It's risky, but it could work."

"I'm lost," Cass whines.

James scowls. "Of course yeh are."

"What if saying the forbidden words don't work?" Pan asks, and it's a legitimate question. My theory is based on one sentence Cass offered and the lore in Wendy Darling's story.

I squeeze Pan's hand. "That's where you come in. You can use your magic to get us out of there if anything goes wrong. I believe in you."

He swallows hard and glances at Emmit. I see the worry in his eyes, but I have faith. Body or no body, he is still the Neverland Shadow. That power is still connected to him. It has to be. He just needs to trust himself.

"It's a start," Emmit says. "We'll improvise if we have to, but I think it's a good plan."

Chapter 26

Cass

I always thought I'd have a big family. One where my mother helped care for my children and my brother was close, causing chaos but happy. I imagined my father standing beside me as we went over the realm maps, discussing which worlds within our multi-verse were in need of help and which we'd choose to rule beside. I pictured meetings with the gods, where we'd forge new alliances and discuss the ways of old.

I thought I'd have a wife at my side whose opinions were firm, but her heart was true. She'd listen to my concerns about Neverland and the neighboring kingdoms with open ears and a guarded heart because she would love our world just as much as me.

That dream was severed the night Belle decided to challenge the gods. She damned herself and all of Neverland to live in a near barren existence. Our people, the friends and family we'd known since birth, were slaughtered. The few Fae our father helped escape have forgotten us. If they haven't, they've turned their backs. Our home has been cast out of the light to fall within the shadows of the underworld.

Neverland rejected all three of us—Belle, Emmit, and myself —as its heirs to the throne. I was denied my birthright as the Island gave it away to an outsider.

Hundreds of years of my life have been nothing but a living hell. All because of Belle's need for power. Her fear of Wendy and the prophecy she held. And now, Wednesday, who, too many mortal years later, brought the seer's words to life.

"Stop crying, you wretched thing!" Belle yells at my daughter.

A thread inside me pulls tight. I didn't expect to fall in love with the little beast. My kind is supposed to be above those mortal emotions. We have the ability to care and nurture, but an unwavering dedication to something besides myself, the willingness to die for her, and to feel Mira's agony when she cried took me by surprise.

I wait for Mira's wail to change. Each pitch and the way she drags out the sound means something different. She's a complex little creature with so much to say without the vocabulary to do so. This cry means she's hungry. The timing is about right. Mira is due for a bottle and a nap, then will likely need to be changed once she wakes.

"Can't handle a baby?" I taunt as I stride into our father's throne room.

It looks the same as it did all those years ago. Father's chair sits at the center of a dais, Mother's beside it, their gilded grace lacking the shine they once held, but still beautiful. My seat was beside Father's, as was Emmit's. Belle was seated beside Mother. Someone has cared for them as there's not a speck of dust, only tarnish from lack of polish.

The grand room still holds the same portraits on the walls. Our family history, captured in paint, spans over a dozen generations. I'm sure the paintings have seen more horrors under Belle's reign than in all the years Neverland has been in existence. I'm grateful the murals can't talk. Father would be so ashamed if he knew the stories they could tell.

Belle's drawn the satin curtains, cutting out what little outside light Neverland has to offer. It makes the room feel colder. Or maybe that's the lingering spirits of everyone who died here.

"Tell me, sister, how do you expect to be queen if you can't control a child?" I taunt her to lure her away from Mira. Belle, while dangerous, is semi-predictable. She's a cat, and I am her prey. I'm counting on her wanting to play with me before delivering the fatal blow.

"With your powers, of course. Ready to die, brother?" As I had hoped, she steps down from the dais and ambles near the center of the room.

"Actually, we had a better idea." Emmit emerges from the shadows of the hallway. He strides into the throne room with his head held high, exuding practiced confidence.

"What a pleasant surprise," Belle says, her smile wide but her words clipped. "I wasn't expecting so much company, but having us all under one roof again is nice. Tell me, brother, what is your plan?"

Emmit tugs on a twine rope attached to Wednesday's wrists. She comes into the light, semi-voluntarily walking to his side, and lets him push her down onto her knees. My cock twitches at the submission. That woman is something extraordinary. If only she hadn't fallen for fucking Peter Pan. I could have made her my wife, the future Queen of Neverland, once I had my island back.

James and Emmit think the Island chose her anyway. I think they're full of shit.

Belle's spine straightens. She licks her lips and glides to the center of the room, leaving a trail of golden dust in her wake. "The precious Darling girl. You, dear, have caused quite the stir on my island."

"A gift," I add. The words feel like fire in my mouth. I'd never give her Wednesday. I did what I had to do to get my kingdom back. Was it ruthless? Yes, but I still care for the girl. At the very least, she's the mother of my child, but in truth, she's more. So much more. "To show our loyalty."

"You were always smarter than you let on, brother." Belle turns her attention back to Wednesday. Her long nails caress the side of Wednesday's face. "I wonder what pretty little things are inside your mind?"

"Belle!" James's voice booms from the hallway. Right on time. We want Belle to have the illusion of power. Too long with the

Darling and we risk her life. Not long enough and she'll see this ruse for what it is. A trap.

"Not now!" Belle hisses.

James ignores her and carries in a hog-tied Peter, or if Wednesday's assumptions are correct, Pan. I must say, I enjoy the sight of him bound, too, but for different reasons. "This one was creeping around the castle."

Belle beams with excitement. "My, my. Two presents in one day. The stars must be favoring me. I'm going to enjoy torturing your precious Darling, Peter. You will watch her bleed and listen to her screams while I—"

"I'm right here, you know," Darling says, right on schedule. "And I gotta say, that doesn't sound appealing."

Belle whirls around, her snarl vicious. "How dare you talk back to me! I am Neverland's Queen. You will quiver in my presence."

Wednesday chuckles. She motions to stand, but Emmit pushes on her shoulder to keep her on her knees. "You think you're scary? That's cute. You're a five-foot-nothing woman who weighs what...a hundred pounds soaking wet? I have seen cats scarier than you."

"Why, you little twit, I will cut your tongue out!" Belle stomps over to Wednesday, her claws out, ready to make good on her threat.

Wednesday doesn't cower in the slightest. She glares at Belle and says, "I'd love to see you try. Especially when I don't believe in fairies."

My sister gasps and takes a step back. Her golden skin pales to the color of snow. She looks from Emmit to me, terror in her eyes. I feel her fear. Those words are the only thing that can give true death to a Fae. It's a power only a few can wield, and Wednesday is one of them. I step forward, prepared to catch Belle as she falls. She might not be the sweet girl I grew up with anymore, but she's still my sister. Despite it all, I will always care for her.

I take another step forward and a fire blooms in my chest. It spreads rapidly until it's all I can feel and consumes my thoughts. I find my sister's face as realization dawns on it. She runs to me as the ice in my veins melts. It hurts more than anything I've ever felt. I scream, unable to keep it inside any longer, until it finally stops.

Everything stops.

CHAPTER 27
Wednesday

It all happens so quickly and there's is nothing I can do. As soon as the words leave my lips, I feel them reach out, cold and greedy, like the hand of death. Only, they don't grab the Fae I intended. They latch onto the Fae furthest from me, the one I hate but care for at the same time. I feel that coldness turn to fire and before I can fully comprehend what's happening, it's too late.

Belle runs toward Cass and screams, "No!" But there is nothing she can do either.

I feel her magic, too, as a heaviness reaches out to blanket her brother. It touches him, giving them an extra second to lock eyes, and then poof. Cass bursts into flames and a heartbeat later is nothing but a pile of ash.

Belle turns to me, her eyes flaring with anger. "You!"

"Think this through, sister," Emmit cautions. He steps between us, his hands out to try and slow her.

Something in my brain whispers for me to run, but I can't move. I'm stuck, frozen with shock. Knowing Cass was alive, I was content with being angry with him. He deserved that anger after everything he's put me through, but I never wanted him to die thinking I hadn't forgiven him. What if I'm the reason his soul is stuck in another form of Neverland? An eternal hell he can't escape because we never turned that page in our story.

"Get out of my way, Emmit!" Belle shoves her brother, but he's as still as a statue.

"Cass is dead," he says calmly. Too calmly. Did he know this would happen? Did he know there was a chance the words would kill either him or Cass? If so, why take the risk? We could have found another way to try and take her down.

"Exactly!" Belle wails. Her cheeks are red with fury, her eyes shiny with unshed tears.

"And where did his magic go? To you?" Emmit's words give Belle pause. She stops her tirade as he looks at Pan. "To him?"

Belle presses her lips into a tight line, letting his words process. Based on how angry Belle is and how pale Pan is, I'm guessing neither of them absorbed Cass's powers, which is what he expected. He may have been Mira's father, but she didn't bless him with any gifts.

"Get to the point," Belle growls.

"My point is that we don't know where the baby's magic will go once both parents are dead." Emmit pauses to let Belle mull over his words. "Do you truly want to risk everything you've worked for because you're angry?"

"He's right," James chimes in. "The Island is already in a state of change because of the girl."

"Exactly," Emmit pushes. "Don't tempt the gods when they've already given you such a precious gift." He gestures to me and Pan.

"There is only one god I fear, brother, and he couldn't care less about Neverland and its magic." She pauses to think. "But it wouldn't hurt to consult the fates. Lock the Darling in the study, as it seems our dungeon needs work."

"Of course, sister." Emmit bows and tugs on the rope that binds my wrists. The knot is a dummy slip. I could escape and run if need be, but I'm trusting Emmit knows what he's doing.

"What about this one?" James asks.

Belle chuffs. "If he had any power left, he would have used it. He's useless now that the child is here. End his life however you see fit, but make it painful."

"Yes, my lady." James grabs Pan by the back of the neck and leads him out of the room.

"Let's go." Emmit shortens the leash between us and

pretends that I am the scum of the Earth. He's convincing enough. Belle leaves us, and Mira, without asking any questions, to go...somewhere within the castle.

I can't help but look at the pile of ash as we walk past what's left of Cass. Tears fill my eyes, but I hold them back. I will not give Belle the satisfaction of seeing me cry. I'm sure she thinks I'm a monster for uttering those horrible words, and maybe I am, but I never wanted this to happen. I knew that coming to Neverland would eventually mean forgiving Cass. Mira would need her father to guide her through the Fae aspects of her life. I figured we'd find a way to co-parent and live peacefully. None of that is possible now.

And it's all my fault.

I follow Emmit, unsure of what to do next. I won't risk saying those words again. Not now that I know their target isn't guaranteed. He leads me to what I'm assuming is the study and opens the door. I step inside. "What now?"

He closes it behind us and turns the lock. "Find something in here that could be useful."

"Like what?"

"I don't know. Anything. Our family history is in there. There's bound to be a clue or something as to what's happened to Belle." He walks to one of the walls filled from floor to ceiling with books and stars skimming over the titles.

I stand beside him, overwhelmed by the hundreds of cloth-bound books. Some have print on the spines, others are bare. From what I can tell, there's no order, and most are written in a language I don't understand. "Haven't you read all of this already?"

"No. Cass was supposed to be king. He spent years studying this shit." Emmit pulls out a red book and flips through the pages. He doesn't find what he's looking for because it's back on the shelf a moment later. "My interest lied elsewhere growing up."

Great. So not only did I prevent Mira from ever knowing her

father, but I also killed the only person who might know how Belle came to be so dark and twisted. I slide down the wall and hide my face in my arms. I don't want to cry, but I can't help it. I'm no closer to getting my daughter back, and I recklessly took a key player off the board. I came to Neverland feeling hopeful, but now all I feel is doubt and worry.

"Hey." Emmit touches my arm. "We both knew the risk of you saying those words. It's okay."

"It's not." I look up but can't meet his gaze. I feel so bad. I don't know how Belle can effortlessly take a life. "I killed him."

Emmit pulls me into a hug and tries to soothe me, but it only makes me feel worse. He lost his brother. I should be comforting him, yet here he is placating the stupid mortal girl. "We have bigger things to worry about. Grieve his loss, but don't let it eat at you."

I nod but make no promises. I have a feeling Cass's death is going to be with me for a long time. "How long will I be in here?"

"For appearance purposes, a few hours. I can't spring you, but if I know a certain captain like I think I do, you'll be out sooner rather than later." Emmit's lips lift into a warm smile. I think the comment about James is supposed to make me feel better, but it just adds a new layer of worry to my back.

"You don't think he'll kill Pan, do you?"

His brows push together and he regards me for the first time as something more than a weak mortal the Island chose. "You know he's not Peter?"

I nod and can't help but wonder what else Emmit knows and has purposely kept secret. "Do you?"

Emmit runs his hand through his hair and sighs. "Did I know? Yes. Do I think he's in danger with James? No, but Pan is struggling to adjust to having a body, especially one without magic."

"Wait, he's not the Neverland shadow anymore?"

"Nope. The Island is changing. With Peter dead—"

"Oh my god! Peter's dead?" No. He can't be. He has to be somewhere on this Island. Peter can't die. He's a legend. The boy who lives forever. The man who stole my life and my heart. He can't be dead. He just can't!

"Fuck, I thought you knew." Emmit lets out a heavy breath and sits back on his heels. "Maybe. Probably. I don't know. All I know is that Pan is Peter, but with no magic. Belle is on a war path with stolen magic. Cass is dead, and now I have to go kiss the bitch's ass." He squeezes my shoulder. "I need you to find something that can help us take down Belle and fast. Can you do that?"

I wipe my nose with the back of my hand. "I can try."

"Good." He stands and looks around the room. "I should go. Belle will be consulting with the fates soon and I want to hear what they have to say. You've got this, Wednesday. I believe in you."

"Thanks," I mutter, trying to be strong, but as soon as the door closes and I'm alone, I crumble.

CHAPTER 28

Neverland once had a shadow. A darkness comprised of the worst parts of myself with infinite powers. It learned to hone all of my anger and resentment, all of the sorrow and regret, and turn it into a strength I never had. It protected our island and, from time to time, was its voice.

A voice I often wished would shut up and leave me alone.

I never understood Pan's constant need to prattle. He could talk for hours and it took me years to figure out how to block the bond to stay sane. Living with another voice in your head is maddening. Eventually, we found a balance, but I understand it now. The desperate need to be heard. For someone to acknowledge your existence. This world is cold and lonely. It's too easy to fall into the darkness and lose yourself when you feel there's no one by your side. But all it takes is for one person to listen to keep your head above water.

Pan had me.

And I have no one.

I don't know how I lost control of my body. One minute, he and I were arguing about how to care for Wednesday and the next, there was darkness. It felt like I fell asleep because when my eyes opened again, I was rejuvenated, but also empty. Literally. I floated like a spirit in the sky at the barrier of Neverland, just outside of its grasp in the land of the living. I could feel Pan drifting away. The bond between us stretched thin, but something pulled me back to the ground. A tinging. A need to find and protect. I thought the sensation had pulled me to my Darling, but I was wrong.

I was called to look after her child. The anomaly of life growing.

Watching Wednesday cry herself to sleep those first few days after Pan left was excruciating. I wanted to hold her and tell her I was still here. My hands went through her body, peppering her skin with goosebumps. I couldn't comfort her, couldn't tell her how much I cared, couldn't let her know I hadn't left her alone, and it was torture.

But all of that changed when the first full moon rose in the sky and the barrier between my world and hers grew thinner. Somehow, she could hear me just as I had heard Pan. It was exhilarating. Not the life I would have chosen for us by any means, but to truly love someone means that you adapt. Life prides itself in throwing curveballs at your face, and the choices it gives are to roll with the punches or die.

I'll be damned if I let our bond die.

Everything changed again when Mira was born. A pulse was sent out into the universe that Wednesday couldn't see, but I was sure could be felt all the way to Neverland. I hoped I was wrong. I hoped the innocent baby girl my Darling had brought into the world would be safe, but even Wednesday knew better. I think she felt the danger even though she didn't know what it was. Her stupid sister didn't understand. She didn't believe Wednesday when anything Neverland-related was spoken.

I often wonder if Darling had been in the room, if she and I could have protected Mira from Cass. The energy is wasted because as I stand unnoticed in the throne room rocking the forgotten child because I know that this is the path Neverland intended me to be on.

Footsteps echo from within the palace corridors. I ready myself to defend the girl despite my limited powers. I don't have nearly the abilities Pan did. I can't summon a storm or corral the animals. I can't wield objects with my mind or bleed into the shadows. But I can guide others, like how I warned Cass about the encroaching fires or how I drew the Darling to his tree house. I can soothe the child, my hands allowed to touch all things related to her, even though they passed through everything else.

Too many days after she first arrived, I fed and changed the girl as if she were my own, without Cass realizing what was happening because he is utterly clueless when it comes to taking care of a child.

Or should I say...was.

I recognize the voices and rub the little one's belly. She's hungry and has cried herself to sleep, something I haven't let happen since the first day Cass brought her into this world.

"Over there!" Xyris's not-so-quiet whisper draws the attention of the others. Scarlett and Aria hug the walls near the entrance. Their swords are drawn, ready to fight if they're caught, while Xyris runs across the room.

If they were smart, one would be guarding the far entrance, too, but I don't sense any danger. No need to alert them of anything just yet.

Xyris sheaths his weapon and reaches into the cradle. He scoops the sleeping Mira into his arms and rests her against his chest. I touch her back, willing her to stay asleep until they breach the walls again. Belle only has a handful of soldiers, all mindless drones she's sucked the life out of. They have no thoughts of their own anymore and exist only to serve her needs. I've never seen them do anything more than stand guard, but I wouldn't put it past her to have whispered contingency orders in their ear if there ever was a breach to occur.

"You'll be safe," I say to the child, and Xyris's gaze lifts. He looks at me, and something stirs inside. "Xyris?"

He blinks and then shakes his head. The small ounce of hope I had that there was someone on this island besides the baby who knew I was here dies. Pan was Neverland's shadow. Seen but not heard. Acknowledged but not feared.

Whereas I am its ghost.

I let them leave, keeping my senses open for any danger they might encounter, and follow the trail to the Darling. She's easy to find, which makes me wonder if it was this simple for Pan. If he was as drawn to Wednesday as I am, he could have known about her rebirth the moment she took her first breath. Something I would love to ask him about, but we aren't connected. Like the Lost and everyone else I've tried to speak with, he can't hear me.

I walk through the closed door and almost through the Darling. She's huddled on the floor, knees pulled to her chest, her head down as tears soak her cheeks. It's a sight I saw too many times back in the land of the living. My heart breaks for her. I don't know if she's mourning the loss of Cass or if there are new traumas burned into her soul since I left. Even though Cass was a motherfucker, I'm sure her sorrow is a mixture of it all. He doesn't deserve her tears, but they will still fall for him because Wednesday is a good person with a big heart. She'll let go of all the pain he caused and focus on the good times when she thinks of him beyond this day.

I crouch down in front of her and, even though I know she can't hear me, I still try to comfort her. That is my curse. Wanting nothing but happiness for this woman and being unable to give it to her. "You know what they say, Darling. What goes around comes around."

Wednesday lifts her head. Those big eyes meet mine, tear-stained red and glossy. "Peter?"

CHAPTER 29

Peter

I stumble back and fall, half expecting to go through the floor. It takes effort to walk and act like I am still myself. Pan never cared. He floated and flew around like a feather in the night, whereas all of this is new to me and I still want to feel like... me.

"Peter?" Wednesday sniffles and her gaze darts around the room. "Is that you?"

"You can hear me?" I ask for the second time today. I don't expect a response. No one can ever hear what I have to say, but that doesn't stop me from being hopeful.

Wednesday's lips lift into the most beautiful smile I've ever seen. It's warm and bright and so full of life. "Yes! Oh gods, Peter, I missed you so much. Emmit said you were dead. Are you dead?" She waits less than a second for me to respond before dropping her face to her hands again. "I'm losing it again. Aren't I?"

I reach Wednesday's arm, expecting it to pass through her like it does every other person I touch in Neverland. To my surprise, my hand holds steady on her skin, goosebumps raising her little blonde hairs.

Wednesday looks up again, her lips parted lightly. "I feel you."

She reaches her hand out and I lean into her touch. I feel her, too. She's warm and soft and damn it, if I had tears, I could cry. I'm not alone in this world anymore, and it makes me so happy that it's my Darling who knows I'm here.

"I want to see you."

"Me too," I tell her.

"Oh, my stars! Peter!" Wednesday lunges forward and wraps her arms around my neck. I fall backward onto the floor, not through it, and hug her back. I don't even get the chance to process that we're hugging before her lips find mine. I thread my fingers through her hair and pull her close. I don't know how this is possible. I don't care either. I'm just glad.

Wednesday laughs as she crawls off me. "How?"

I wipe the tears from her cheeks, hoping happy ones are mixed in with the sad, and say, "I don't know. Neverland magic, I guess."

She sits cross-legged on the floor across from me. Her eyes trail over my body, taking in every inch. I hope it's the same as before and that she still likes what she sees. It's not like I have a reflection anymore to know what I look like. "But you're not a shadow."

"No, I'm not." And never was. "I called myself the ghost of Neverland for a minute. It was funny until it wasn't." Being a ghost is more depressing than it is funny. Maybe if I could have scared Cass or tormented Belle it would have been more fun, but all I could do was look after the little one. A task I am grateful to have been given, but sometimes I wish I could do more.

"But you're here."

"I know."

"No, Peter." Wednesday scampers to one side of the room and empties a silver serving tray resting on an end table. She wipes the dust away with her shirt and holds the metal up so I can see my reflection. "You're actually here."

"That's not how it works." I am grateful she can see me too, but I have no body for the image to reflect. I try to tell her as much, but then I see myself. The warm glow of my cheeks. The dark hue of my hair. I reach up to touch my face and even the tattoos on my arms are there. The clothes I wore in the world of the living, simple jeans and a short-sleeved shirt are as clear as the day is bright. I touch the fabric of my shirt, and it lifts. It's not a part of my body anymore, but on it.

I lunge at the Darling and lift her off her feet. She laughs as I lean down and claim her lips again. I kiss her until she's breathless, then move to her neck, and she lets out a sigh. That sound will be my undoing. If we weren't under the roof of a psychopath, I'd take Wednesday now and make up for all the time I've lost, but there are other more important matters to attend to.

Despite wanting to stay in her arms forever, I take a step backward to create distance between our bodies and try to fit the pieces together. "This shouldn't be possible."

"Neverland shouldn't be possible," she says with a laugh, "but here we are."

I can't argue with her logic, but something still seems amiss. If I have my body again, where is Pan? What happened to him?

The door handle jiggles, ending any further conversation. Wednesday looks at me with wide eyes. I'm not supposed to be here, but maybe I am to keep the Darling safe now that the little one is in good hands.

I back myself against the wall, hiding myself from the intruder's sight once the door opens. I ball my fists, ready to fight. There is no hum of magic in my veins anymore. I don't feel the Island's warning, just like I can't feel Pan's presence. I'm not worried. I lived most of my life here without magic. I don't need the Island's help to kick someone's ass.

Wednesday takes a step back and grabs a pillow. It was the closest thing to her, so I understand reaching for it, but the down-stuffed fabric isn't going to save her. Then again, she's got me now. So, I guess her choice of weaponry doesn't matter.

"Really, Sunshine?" my brother asks, humor in his tone when he enters the room. "What are yeh going to do? Smother me to death?"

"Asshole," Wednesday teases as she throws the pillow at his face.

James effortlessly swats it away. He peeks into the hallway

again, then extends his hand. "Everything is in order, but we need to leave."

"What about Mira?"

"Xyris and the girls grabbed her a few minutes ago." I step out of my hiding place and tuck my hands into my pockets. It's a strange sensation having them again, both pockets and hands.

"I left yeh at the boat. How did you...?" James's brows knit together as he takes in the subtle differences between me and my shadow.

"Not Pan," I say because there's no other explanation.

James processes what I said and then grins. "Fuckin' brilliant, but there's no time to explain. We need to leave."

He steps forward and takes Wednesday's hand in his. Something twists inside me as I watch their fingers intertwine. I see it, just like I did all those years ago, the bond between my brother and the woman who holds my heart. I don't hold it against her if she's fallen for him or anyone else. I've been a ghost in this world for weeks. The stars only know how many years it's been for her in the land of the living, but seeing that she's moved on stings.

Wednesday turns to look at me as she and James pass. She takes my hand and smiles, pulling me along with them. A strange glimmer of hope that the Darling could love us both warms my veins. Wendy would never allow herself the satisfaction. It was always one or the other, even though we both knew her heart was torn. James got the bulk of Wendy's love while I got the stolen moments and scraps, but for me, it was enough.

I follow her down the dark tunnels beneath the castle, holding her hand while she holds James's. Only it doesn't feel like I'm a tag-along. Wednesday holds me tight and something tells me that this time around, things with the Darling will be different.

CHAPTER 30

James

"I'm putting my foot down, James," Smee shouts from the deck of the ship, hands on her hips.

We should be the last to arrive if everything went according to plan. Xyris and the girls should already be on board with the baby. I hand-delivered Pan to his quarters—that situation is a mindboggling miracle that needs to be addressed, but not now—and Emmit stayed behind, working as a spy behind enemy lines.

"And when the hell did that one leave the ship?" she screeches, pointing to Peter. "I told Rodgers to keep an eye on him at all times."

I fight a frown and work to keep my face as expressionless as possible. I understand Smee is concerned. Bringing everyone here is a risk, but it's one I'm willing to take. Outside of the small plot of land Cass saved, and Belle's castle in the mountain, Neverland is in pieces. Our ship is the only safe space for survivors. Not just Peter's friends, but ours too. We found thirteen survivors throughout the cove, all with various stages of burns to their bodies and so many more that were unsaveable. I can't begin to understand the pain my crew is feeling. They carried on the search while I went back for Wednesday, but I'm sure the weight of our loss hangs heavy.

"I have!" Rodgers protests. "He's right here."

Smee turns to look over her shoulder. I know she'll find Pan obediently beside Rodger because that's what I ordered him to do. Be a wallflower. Cause no waves while I'm gone, or he wouldn't be welcome to stay once I brought Wednesday back. My brother's shadow was more amicable than I expected. The beast is relatively tame for a creature that held all of Peter's darkest desires.

I cross the plank, guiding us from what's left of our dock onto the deck. Wednesday is behind me, with Peter following her. I hold her hand while he steadies her waist. There's no chance she will fall into the water. I've worked too hard to let Triton claim her. Stars above only know what he'd do with a soul as pure as hers.

"There are two of them!" Smee shrieks. Her blatant observation draws the attention of everyone on the deck, which is more people than I'm used to seeing aboard the old girl. Majority of the pirates are below, resting in their quarters, but there are four faces I recognize up here waiting. Them, plus six of the crew, and Peter's Lost make for a crowd to witness our arrival.

"Have I not mentioned that Peter is a twin?" I offer light-heartedly. I need to speak to Wednesday, Peter, and Pan alone to see if they agree with my theory before I offer it to listening ears. God knows I don't need to instill false hope into anyone at this point.

I help Wednesday navigate the steps onto the deck. She offers me a brief smile before her gaze searches the crowd. She finds her treasure, happily tucked into her friend's arms, and runs to the Lost. I watch, feeling my own form of joy as she reunites with her child. The moment is bittersweet because I remember the days when my boys were young. Wendy loved them with every inch of her being. She glowed with pride every time they were around and wilted when we washed ashore without them.

I don't think Wendy realized that losing John and Michael broke me, too. She was too deep in her own grief to realize that I shut off my pain to protect her. We had a handful of survivors with no food, no shelter, and a pissed-off Peter who offered no help. I had to shoulder all the burden, and when I finally reached a point where I could open up and be the emotional support Wendy needed, she was gone.

I'd lost my wife.

I'd lost my kids.

My brother hated me and pulled away.

I couldn't even be mad at him because it was all my fault. If I hadn't taken us on the stupid voyage to try and find an uncharted island to bring Wendy's stories to life we would never have fallen into the whirlpool. My boys would have lived full lives and my wife would have grown to old age by my side.

But giving Wednesday the gift of finding what was lost and reuniting her with her child eases the guilt I feel for what I did to Wendy.

"This is going too far, Cap," Smee insists. "I won't allow it."

I drag my gaze from Wednesday's reunion to my first mate. Anger rolls off of her in waves, and she is trying my patience. I never corrected her for disrespecting me before the Darling and I left for Neverland, and that error is coming back to bite me in the ass. "Mind yourself, Smee."

"No!" she shouts and takes a challenging step toward me. "We trust you to do what's best for the crew. That's why you're our captain, but you've gone too far. The Lost have a target on their backs."

"Be careful with yehr words," I warn.

"There's not one Neverking, but two, and you've captured them both. I understand they are your brothers, but the girl and the child..." Smee pauses to glance at Wednesday.

I shake my head, wishing she'd shut her trap and listen to reason. By the laws of our code, mutiny is punishable by death. Despite being a fool, Smee thinks she's looking out for the crew. I won't hurt her for doing what she thinks is best, but I'll have to punish her. If not, my hold as captain will slip. "Think hard, old friend. You're about to do something that can't be undone."

"They are who Belle wants most," she continues, not having heard my warning. "Having them here is a death sentence for us all. They can't stay."

"Every person on this ship is now a member of our crew. As

the captain, it's my right to allow them into our home, and as my first mate, it's your job to see they feel welcomed."

"She doesn't belong here!" Smee insists. Her shouting startles the baby, and she cries.

I can take the verbal lashing, and I can handle the beratement of Wednesday, but hearing the child cry does something to me. My anger seized control and I finally snap. "That's where yehr wrong! Wednesday has always belonged here! Her home is by my side, and I will always offer it to her. She is my wife in this life and the next. Beyond life and death. Those were my vows and I will stick by them until the day my soul rots and there is nothing left. Her child. Her friends. They all fall under that umbrella because they are an extension of her. Yeh don't have to like my decisions, Smee, but as yehr captain yeh have to accept them."

"I can't." Smee looks at me with tears in her eyes. It hurts because she is my friend, the closest person to me in this world as much as I want to, I can't comfort her.

"Then this can't be yehr home anymore."

"I've been by your side for years, James." Her voice cracks with emotion. Her heart breaks before my eyes, and still, I hold my ground. "You were supposed to choose me."

"It was never a choice. It is and will always be Wednesday. I'm sorry, I thought yeh knew."

"I'm going to grab my things."

"Smee..." I reach for her arms, regret sinking in. Maybe I was too harsh. Maybe if given time, she'd understand.

Smee twists out of my reach and shakes her head. "Don't. You've done enough."

She walks with her head held high to the stairs that lead below deck. I feel terrible, but there are more pressing matters at hand. We still have to deal with Belle. Once she's out of the picture and Neverland is safe, I'll find Smee again. Once a pirate, always a pirate. We'll get through this as we have done everything else.

Wednesday puts her hand on my arm. "I'm sorry, James."

"I'm not." I stroke the soft blonde hairs of her daughter's head. The little thing seems at peace in her mother's arms. It radiates warmth into the air. The girl is pure magic. Even an idiot can sense that she's special. Which means it won't take long for Belle to realize she's gone. "But now isn't the time to dwell on my loss. We need to talk." I look at my brother and his shadow come to life. "All of us."

"Agreed." Peter steps forward. "Lead the way, Captain."

CHAPTER 31
Wednesday

Mira is the most beautiful baby I've ever seen.

She's grown since I last saw her. Her legs are a little chunkier and her belly is a touch rounder but, essentially, she looks almost the same as the day I had her. Perfect.

I haven't put her down since boarding the Jolly Roger. I know people say that holding a baby too much makes them clingier and more dependent on their parents, but those people, whoever they are, never lost their child. They don't know the fear that comes with wondering if your baby is all right. They don't understand the constant worrying, and they can't imagine the relief when that nightmare comes to an end.

I will hold my daughter and I will love her every second of every day that she lets me because each minute we have together is a gift.

I rock her back in forth. James was ready for her before I even came back to the ship. I don't know how he did it, but he had a rocking chair, cradle, and a changing table crafted and moved into his room. In a span of hours, he rescued the injured, saved Peter and me, and still found time to prepare for a infant. This man blows my mind in the best of ways.

"Can I hold her?" Pan asks.

Fear wraps itself around my bones. The last time I let my baby girl go she was stolen from me. I want to tell him no and kick everyone out of the room, but this is Pan. My Shadow. My friend. I know with full confidence that he and everyone else in here would die before hurting me or Mira. I'm not alone anymore. I'm with my family again and the only way we're going to keep Mira safe is by trusting each other.

I stand and lay her in his arms. It's nerve-wracking to let her go, but watching the emotions play out on Pan's face is fascinating. Fear. Excitement. Then pure adoration.

"You're good at that," I say, and Pan beams up at me. I don't know if he existed in the years John and Michael were alive. By Neverland logic—which is that anything is possible—there is a chance that the memories of Peter holding and loving his nephews have been imprinted on Pan's soul because he is a natural. Mira hasn't woken since the handoff and she looks more than content in his arms.

"Can I address the elephant in the room?" Scarlett says. "How the hell are there two of you? And don't even try that twins-bullshit. I know Peter only has one brother. Your crew might be fine accepting that you've kept secrets from them, but Peter told us everything."

"I have a theory." James walks to the liquor cabinet and pours himself a glass of scotch. He takes his time, letting the flavors roll on his tongue before swallowing. "But I want to hear how it happened."

"There have always been two of us." Pan hands Mira back to me. She's warm and smells like morning dew and sea spray. I set her in the cradle, torn between looking at her forever and joining the conversation. The choice is made for me when Pan says, "But you all have only ever acknowledged him."

"So, you're Peter's Shadow?" Aria pokes his arm.

I glare at her and come to his side. I understand that he is a lot to take in, and I have had time to see Pan in person before today, but there is a way to handle the distrust and curiosity while remaining tactful.

"Yes."

"Then how are you here?" Xyris asks, and that is one question I am curious about, too.

I understand that Peter and Pan are two separate people. I

know they share one space when they are on Earth. Pan was a voice in Peter's mind, but Peter was the one in control of his body... Until Pan became the dominant personality and Peter went to the back burner, but I thought things would go back to normal when they returned to Neverland.

"The better question," Pan turns to Peter, "is how are you here? This is your body. How did you get one of your own?"

"I don't know. When I came back to Neverland, I wasn't a shadow like you. I couldn't talk to anyone or control the Island. I had lesser magic, but it was only helpful in protecting Mira." He glances at the crib and it dawns on me that I couldn't hear him anymore because he left me to take care of her. "Wherever she went, I went. I was there when Cass died. I saw you," He looks to Xyris. "And the girls take the baby. I knew she would be safe with you, so I went looking for Wednesday, and the next thing I knew, I was me again. Flesh and bone."

"That's how it went on my end, too," I add. "Emmit knew Pan was in Peter's body. He said Peter died, and I... well, I lost my shit. I was crying when I thought I heard his voice. I wanted so badly for him to be real and to be with me, and then *poof* he was."

"If there were any doubts that you are Neverland's new queen, they should be gone," James says proudly. All eyes turn to him as he sips his crystal glass filled with brown liquor.

"Come again?" Aria asks.

"Cass was an ice wielder, Emmit is a healer, Belle, before she became corrupt by blood magic, was sky bound and could control the sky. All of the royal Fae had powers that tied them to the Island. Peter, being human-born, couldn't wield the Neverland magic, so his soul was split and Pan became a shadow self. Each legacy of the Neverking is given a gift, and you, Sunshine, by being Mira's mother, were given one, too. The gift of life."

Pan crosses his arms and shares a glance with Peter. "Go on."

"Only one person has ever existed in Neverland with a beating heart." James holds his glass and points to me. "The same person who insisted the Island wasn't Belle's and made it rain so as not to let it die. A beautiful, powerful woman who willed Peter back to life."

"I wasn't dead," he chides.

"But you weren't alive either. You were caught in between, like all of us. Only your prison lacked shape and forced you into isolation. Do you disagree?" James prods.

"No," Peter mumbles.

"Point proven. Wednesday wanted you to be with her and so you were." James saunters over to Mira's cradle. "But most importantly, let's not forget about the child. The true heir to Neverland, a soul born of both worlds that should never have existed because the Fae can't breed with humans and yet, here she is." James tosses back the last of his drink and sets the tumbler down. "Neverland chose you, Wednesday. Not Wendy. Not any other soul. You."

James's statement is a lot to process, and I've heard half the speech before. He comes before me, drops down to one knee, and takes my hand. "The Island knew it needed a savior. It couldn't have picked a better one."

"I cannot be the savior." I cross my arms and hug myself. "I can't fight or fly or do anything useful. I am just a mother who wanted her child back. Saviors are special, and I'm just...me."

Peter steps in front of me as James rises to his feet. "You don't honestly think that? Do you, Darling?"

I shrug.

He pulls me into a hug, one I needed but damn sure wasn't about to ask for. Today has been too much. Cass died. I was a prisoner. Peter went from not quite dead to very alive, and now this. A declaration that I'm destined to save us all.

I can't.

I don't know how.

"Even on your darkest days, when you feel worthless, never forget that you are everything." Peter cups my cheeks and wipes away my tears with his thumb. "I crossed through time and space for you. As did Pan and James. Do you think we'd do that for just anyone?"

"And we felt it the moment Peter brought you to Neverland," Scarlett adds.

"There was a ripple in the air, a legit wave across the water the other night. We just didn't know what it was," Xyris says. "But it was you. You changed everything, and I think that's why Belle has gone a little crazy."

"She's always been crazy." Aria snickers. "But she's definitely amped it up a few levels since we last saw you."

Someone twists the handle of James's double doors. When they don't open, he pounds against the stained glass over and over until James nods to Xyris to open them. The two seconds of tension that fills the room is thick. The boys' stances change, readying themselves to fight, while the girls step closer to the wall, out of the way.

Pan puts himself between Mira and whoever is outside while Peter protectively stands in front of me.

Emmit rushes in, panting, covered in sweat. There's a general breath of air released as the tension falls away, until he says, "We don't have a lot of time. She's coming."

CHAPTER 32
Peter

"Stay with the baby," I tell Pan. This may be James's ship, and he may be used to giving the orders, but this is my fight and my family on the line.

"Why?"

"Because Belle doesn't know there are two of us and your hand-to-hand combat skills are probably shit considering you haven't had hands long."

If something were to happen to me, Mira would need a guardian, Wednesday will need a partner to help her, and I need to guarantee that at least one of us survives.

"I'm not leaving her," Darling insists. She grips the edge of Mira's cradle so tightly that her knuckles turn white. I nod, understanding her choice, and don't hold it against her. She was robbed of her child once and fought tooth and nail to have her again. She shouldn't be on the battle front, anyway. Wars aren't fought by kings and queens. Wednesday is our queen. She shouldn't have to risk her life for a world that's only just become hers. That's our job.

"All the more reason one of you should stay." James hands me a sword. A thin piece of metal with a black handle. The smallest in the bunch he carries, but just as deadly as the rest because it's made from iron, not steel. As are the daggers he's strapped to his chest. "I don't care who stays, but I can't protect the girls and the ship. I need help on all fronts."

"I won't let anything hurt them." Pan takes a sword, but it's clear he's never held one.

I adjust his grip and then look around, making sure everyone is armed. We are an army of six going to war with a woman who singularly has the power of ten, if not more. The odds are against us in every way. If I were a believer in the gods, I'd pray, but they abandoned Neverland long ago. I can't see them helping us now.

"It's been three days since Belle last fed." James tucks two more daggers into the holster on his chest and slips another into his boot. "Her dust will be weak, lasting minutes if not seconds, and every burst she throws will weaken her."

"How do you know?" Scarlett asks. She looks uncomfortable holding her weapon. I scan the room and find two other swords in a barrel behind James's chart table. These are smaller, almost half the size, but they'll be lighter. I offer a trade, her heavy sword for these. Scar hesitates but then wordlessly switches.

"Because I was the last soul she fed on," James admits. His brows furrow as he tries to hide his shame. His gaze finds mine for the first time since entering this room. To everyone else, he looks angry, but I know my brother. He's hurting both inside and out, and I wonder why I never saw it before. He didn't have to sacrifice himself. He could have sent one of his pirates to bleed for his former queen. It crosses my mind that I may have misunderstood his place among the pirates.

"The marks," Wednesday gasps. "Are those from her?"

"Poison." He nods.

Emmit touches James's markings and wrinkles his nose. "This isn't poison. I could take some of it if it were. This is magic. I think she bonded with you."

"What does that mean?" I ask.

There are only two types of bonds the Fae can create. An imprint, where they siphon energy and life from their bonded, and the mating bond. Both options require the bonded to sacrifice, but only one might work in our favor.

"I'm not sure." Emmit casts a glance at me, and I read the silent message. *We need to talk.*

"Everybody ready?" I ask. There's a murmur of yeses and nods, but in truth, none of us are prepared. For the first time since coming to Neverland, the Lost face death. Be it now by a sword or later by the hands of a tyrannical queen, if we don't fight it's imminent.

Wednesday hugs each one of us as we leave the room, offering "Be safe" and "I'd better see you after this" to us all. Her words are kind, but don't pierce the emotional armor our family has put up.

James is next. He takes Wednesday's chin between his fingers and pulls her in to kiss her goodbye. Pan looks away, but I can't. It's obvious that she cares for him, maybe even loves him. I can't help but wonder if the feelings are solely hers or if they are mixed with Wendy's emotions. I guess it doesn't matter. The original Darling loved us both. This one can too.

"The light in my darkness," James says against her lips. "Thank you."

Wednesday nods and wipes a tear from her cheek. James doesn't linger. He turns and heads out onto the deck to give a pep talk to his crew. He leaves the door open, wordlessly reminding me to join him. As if I could forget.

"This isn't fair," Wednesday says. She sniffles and tries to fight a new wave of tears. "I just got you. Both of you."

"And you will always have us," I insist. I can only imagine how difficult this must be for her. Walking away, even knowing that she and Mira will be safe and that Pan is the final leg of defense should anything happen to us out there, is still one of the hardest things I will ever do. But I am doing it for her.

"All of us. One of us. Whatever you choose, we're here for you," my other half adds.

Even without the bond connecting us, Pan knows where I stand. It's clear Wednesday's heart is full and only a bastard would force her to choose. It's not ideal. I want her to myself, but with Pan living and breathing, that's not possible. My brother is just another layer to bring into the mix I'll have to adjust to as well. "Agreed."

"I should have told you about me and James," Wednesday

says, ashamed. "There just hasn't been time and I honestly wasn't sure how."

I pull her close and try not to dwell on the fact that this could be the last time I hold my Darling. I wish we could have had the reunion we deserve, but the stars didn't favor us in that respect. Still, if this is all I get, I am grateful. "Hey. It's okay. We aren't making you choose. I just figured that whatever happens out there, you should know I love you. I can't remember if I've said that yet."

"I love you, too, Peter." She holds me tight, then reaches a hand out for my shadow. "And I love you, Pan."

"I know, Darling," he says resoundingly, then looks at me. "I'll guard them with my life."

Ah, my cue to go. Seems my shadow can still read me despite us losing our bond to communicate. "I know you will."

I shut the door and listen for the clink of the lock behind me. *She will be safe*, I remind myself. *They all will be.*

James's ship is sprinkled with soldiers. He's arranged the crew and the Lost in a fanned-out triangle, as if he were at war again, with him at the point near the bridge. Emmit stands on the port side, waiting for Belle to arrive.

He doesn't wave or motion for me to join him, but I know that's where I need to go next. "Tell me about the bond," I whisper.

"I have a theory," he says, "but you're not going to like it."

I force a laugh because that is the undertone of my life. Nothing has worked out the way I hoped, and I've had to adapt. My father never regarded me as someone worth his time. The love of my life married and fell for my brother. My nephews— one of whom I would have bet my life on as being mine—were ripped from this world while I was forced to live forever in a realm constantly being invaded by a crazy, magic-hungry fairy. Me not liking something isn't new. "I don't like anything when it comes to your sister."

"If Belle dies, James might, too."

My smile falls and my heart sinks to the bottom of the ocean. James may be a lot of things, half of which I don't like, but he is the only true family I have left. It's taken years for us to find our way back together. I'm not ready to say goodbye. "Could you bring him back?"

"From death?" Emmit rubs his chin and mulls over his words. "No, but depending on how *she* dies...maybe. The swords are iron cast. If we stab her in the right place, it could kill her without taking James's life too. It'll hurt like a bitch, but I can delay his death and take the pain away, and after a few days heal him to where it never happened."

"Got it. Avoid the heart," I say as Belle emerges through the smoke with ten mindless soldiers, all dressed for battle and one painfully familiar pirate. "James isn't going to take Smee's betrayal well."

"I figured. Thought it best he sees her true nature for himself. No one wants to hear that someone they love stabbed them in the back."

I know the feeling. I loved Cass like a brother and he betrayed me. He tried to take the only thing I've ever wanted and end her life. That kind of backstabbing never heals, but the ache eventually shifts to a dull throb. Especially now that he's dead. "I'm sorry about Cass."

"Don't be." Emmit stares at the treeline and watches his sister approach. She follows behind her line of soldiers, walking in a gilded dress, shining like the sun herself and just as deadly. "The scales will always be balanced, one way or another. I warned him his plan was shit. He didn't listen when I tried to talk him out of it."

"You knew he wanted to kill Wednesday?" Anger burns my throat. I swallow the heat, but only because today isn't a day to make new enemies. I need him by my side. Even if he, too, can't be fully trusted anymore. "Why didn't you say something?"

"Because I would not pick one brother over another." He looks at me and claps his hand on my shoulder. "You, Pan, and I are born from the same magic. Wednesday is, too, and her child is the purest of us all. My weight in the battle for Neverland was even; I couldn't pick sides, but now it's swayed. Belle threatens to destroy my home and what's left of my family. I can't sit by and let it happen."

I grunt, wanting to hold onto that anger, but let it go. I understand. He and I may be brothers, but Cass was blood. He couldn't betray him, and I guess I should be grateful that he didn't help. Although, now that I think about it, Emmit never offered to help heal Wednesday when she was sick either. This explains why. "I appreciate you siding with us, but you're still a mother fucker for letting things get this far."

Emmit chuckles and shoots me a knowing look. "Wednesday's destiny was written before you even existed. I did nothing but let fate guide her path."

"So, you're saying this fight is all a part of Neverland's plan?"

"I feel like it is, which is why I'm not worried. Today will go how it's meant to." He winks and draws his sword. It's nearly time.

I ready my stance and do the same. I wish I had Emmit's confidence. Fear, something I rarely felt before bringing the Darling into my life, tethers itself to me. I glance back at James's quarters and Wednesday peeks through the curtains. I wish she would stay out of sight, but I don't fault her. I'm sure she's just as nervous as we are.

Belle's soldiers run up the plank and spill onto the ship. They fan out, protecting their queen as she boards the Jolly Roger.

Our numbers are close, but most of James's crew is readied to fight below deck, tasked with protecting the injured.

I take a deep breath and walk to stand beside my brother. This is it. The moment we live and claim Neverland for ourselves, or we die.

CHAPTER 33
Wednesday

I run to the window as soon as Peter shuts the door. Pan locks it behind him, as if the tiny metal latch is enough to stop the crazy Fae princess. It's not. If she wants in this room, she'll get in. That I have no doubt.

I pull the curtain aside and peek out. My friends and James's family stand on the deck. Ready. Waiting.

My heart races with anticipation, but I can only imagine how nervous they are. We have an idea of what Belle brings to the table, though I'm sure she has at least one surprise up her sleeve... unless she feels this battle is a waste of time and that it will end quickly.

I hope not. I know I said I would protect my daughter, but I don't know if I can stand here and watch everyone I care about die. If they fall, I'm going out there. James thinks I'm the savior, so that's what I'll do. Save them if they need me.

I hope they don't need me.

"You should get back." Pan reaches for my arm. His touch is gentle yet commanding. "We don't want Belle to see you."

"If Mira is as magical as everyone thinks she is, Belle won't need to see my face to know where we are." She'll be drawn to her. All the more reason to stay put. Just in case, but I'm torn. Half of my heart is in here, safe. While the other half is out there ready to die for me.

Peter walks to the center of the deck and stands beside James, who is dressed to kill. Literally. He has a sword in each hand and a dozen daggers strapped to his body. Peter twists his wrist, showcasing that his singular weapon is just as deadly.

"Well, well, well." Belle's gaze skirts across the deck. I watch her attention bounce from each one of our men to the next, probably counting us and weighing her odds, before focusing on James. Fire flares in her eyes, but her words are as sweet as honey, thick with condescending undertones and meant to cut. "How predictably disappointing. I worried your ties to Peter would come between us one day."

"There was never an us!" James growls.

I wish I could see his face, to read if he truly means the words. I've put the pieces together. I know he and Belle have been intimate, and while I shouldn't be jealous, I am. I don't like knowing her hands have touched his body, and I hate that her teeth have ravaged his skin. She's a parasite. One I pray he never had feelings for.

"Awe." She covers her heart with her hands. "You wound me. Here I thought we had something special."

James chuffs and challenges her. He raises his arm and points a sword at her face. One of her soldiers hunches down low, preparing to launch himself at James if given the word. My captain pays him no mind as he addresses the Fae. "You used me, just like you used all the souls in Neverland, but not anymore."

"Leave, Belle. You aren't welcome here," Emmit adds. Belle's gaze slices to her brother. She scowls, realizing his deceit, but holds her tongue.

"On this boat or our Island," Peter adds, driving their statement home.

That seems to tip her over the edge, the three of them united. She stomps her foot and yells, "I am Neverland's Queen! How dare you disrespect me!"

"Not anymore, you aren't." James's words are cold and cruel. He leaves no room for argument in the statement. I half expect him to fling a dagger at her heart and end the battle before it begins, but beneath his rough exterior, James is kind. If he can avoid bloodshed, he will. "Go, Belle, while you still can."

"You won't kill me, James. You can't," she says with a snicker.

In one swift movement, he hands a sword to Peter and grabs a dagger from the holster on his chest. It flies through the air and sinks itself into Belle's shoulder. She pulls it out, and blood drips off the golden petals that make up her dress. "You're a fool, James Panning!

I can't see James's face, but I'm sure he's got a wicked grin as he says. "That was a warning. My next dagger will be at your heart."

"Guards!" Belle screeches. "Kill them all, but leave the captain and the baby for me." A murderous look glints across her face as she searches the ship. She finds me a second later and smirks. I step back from the window and grab my sword.

"What happened?" Pan asks. He pushes the curtain aside with one finger and peeks out. I don't need to look to know what he sees. Our friends, the Lost and the Pirates, engaged in a battle.

"She's coming," I warn him.

"No." He shakes his head. "She's not. She's just standing there. Watching."

I make my way back to the window, this time with my sword in hand. Not that I know how to use it, but I can swing a base-ball bat. If need be, I can severely hurt someone. Once. Because I doubt I'll get my sword back once it's in someone.

Not like the Panning brothers. Stars above, they are merci-less. They swing and strike and stab every soldier that comes at them, but Belle's souls are monsters. Peter's sword cuts the head off of a red-haired woman, but she doesn't fall. She swings blindly, attacking without yielding. Aria tries to push away a set of legs bent on kicking and stomping her to death. Scarlett runs from an arm that is creepily *Thing* like. Everyone either fights a body or part of one, if not more. The scene is maddening, but not messy. The souls don't bleed like the Lost and Pirates do.

One of the souls lunges for James. He jumps back, avoiding being stabbed by a one-armed zombie, and finds the edge of another monster's sword. The metal slashes his arm, and Belle screams. Bright red blood drips from his shoulder down to his wrist. The gash is two inches long and I don't know how deep, and Belle has one in the exact same place.

"I said leave that one alone!" she shouts.

There's a change in the air and a cold chill that slithers to all corners of the ship. Time slows to almost half speed. I see it, the moment Peter puts the dots together. It's seconds after me.

"What are you doing?" Pan asks as I reach for the locks on the door.

"Let me out," I say, unable to twist and pull and make my fingers work. I need to get out there. I need to save him and stop Peter before it's too late. "Let me out!"

Pan flips the lock and I yank the door open, then step out into the madness. There may not be blood, but the smell coming off of Belle's soldiers is nauseating. I hold my breath and look for Peter. He's here, somewhere. I can feel him. I just... Can't... there!

I run into the center of the madness. I don't have a sword or any way to protect myself if one of the monsters were to notice me but adrenaline has me dogging blades and weaving between fights as I span the length of the deck.

I'm almost to him.

James shoves one of Belle's soldiers, a creature with no head and one arm away. He sees me running to him and stops fighting. "Sunshine?"

"James!" I shout, but I'm too late.

Chapter 34
Wednesday

Peter comes out of nowhere, his body as stealthy as the Shadow, Pan, used to be and as swift as Cass. He takes his sword and shoves it through James's stomach, then rips it out. "I'm sorry."

"No!" I scream as my captain, my unexpected savior, a man I never expected to love, falls to his knees and blood pours out of his mouth. I catch him and ease him to the ground.

One by one, Belle's army falls around us. There isn't a single soul of hers intact. Carved and cut torsos cease fighting while limbs go limp. Metal clanks against the teak as her soldiers finally die.

I don't feel relief that the battle is over because all I can think about is James. I stroke his face and hold him to my chest. He coughs, spitting blood as he gasps for air and the sound of his struggling breaths rip me to pieces.

"It's okay," I tell him. "Everything will be okay."

"You stole everyone I've ever loved. I hate you," Peter says from across the ship. He stares at Belle, who's in just as bad of shape as James. She holds her stomach, trying to close the wound, but crimson leaks out of her. She's bleeding too much to survive, which means...

"Emmit!" I cry as Peter's blade rises into the air. I look away, searching for our friend. He steps forward after a *thump* rolls behind me. "Can you help him?" I ask, refusing to look at Belle.

Emmit takes in James's condition. He has a long gash on one shoulder, deep enough to see bone. The stab wound on his stomach is open and leaking, and a new line of red gathers around James's neck.

Emmit shakes his head, worry wrinkling his face. "I can't take all this on. Not without risking my life."

"You have to try," I beg, my voice cracking. That line, the little one that matches Belle's injury darkens. Whatever happens to one, happens to the other. Peter knew and still he killed her. He knew she was hurt and that we could have found another way, and still, he took her life. If James dies because of his selfish impulsiveness, I'll never forgive him.

"My magic will only drag out the inevitable." Emmit shoots Peter a wicked glare but places his hand on James. "But I can ease his pain so you can say goodbye."

Smee runs across the dock bridge and drops to her knees beside us. She didn't fight her old crew. She led Belle and her soldiers to us but didn't raise a sword against her family. Her morals are fucked, following a twisted line, but she never broke the code James laid out for her. "I'm sorry," she cries, falling apart beside him. "You weren't supposed to get hurt."

"It's okay, Smee. I forgive you." James coughs and more blood pools out of the corner of his mouth. It's a deep, dark purple, pulled from the furthest points of his body. His skin loses its sun-kissed hue as a cold sweat blankets him.

I wipe the blood from his cheek with my shirt sleeve, refusing to accept what is coming. "No! This isn't okay. You're not allowed to die!"

James doesn't have much time left. I can feel it, just as purely as I can feel my bond with Mira. He looks at Peter and croaks, "Take care of her."

"We will," Pan says in unison with Peter. He looks down at us, a frown pulling at his lips, showing so much more than Peter, who seems to have shut us all off.

James's breaths slow. I cradle him to my chest, not caring about the blood ruining my clothes as my tears that flow freely. He's worthy of each one shed. This man was nothing but kind to me. He offered me friendship when I ventured into his cove, unaware of who he was and what our meeting meant. He journeyed across the universe to find me and bring me back to Neverland. He stuck by my side, his belief in me never faltering, even when I didn't believe in myself.

He's a good man that I will mourn and love and, dammit, he doesn't deserve to die!

"You can't die. I won't let you. Please," I beg as another second passes between each inhale. One turns into two and then three until there are too many seconds to count.

I wipe my eyes with the back of my arm, the only part of me not covered in James's blood, and look up at Emmit. "Tell me how this works."

"How what works?"

"My gift. James thinks I can bring things to life. How do I do it? How does this magic work?"

Emmit stops touching James and rubs the back of his neck. He's quiet for a beat and then sighs. "It's different for everyone. I have to touch people to heal them. Belle's moods affected the weather. And Cass...his magic came on demand."

"Well, I'm an emotional mess, touching James, and I demand he comes back to me." I fall over him again. This pain hurts so much more than losing Cass. Perhaps it's because we shared a bond, or maybe it's related to our vows. In this life and the next. Next not being an option if you die in Neverland, but the dam he built inside me that filled the holes Peter and Pan left has been ripped open.

"Darling," Peter coos. He reaches for my shoulder to try and comfort me, but I shift out of his touch. I don't want to hate him, but this is his fault. He took someone I care about away.

"No!" I can't listen to him say James is gone. I won't. I'm the savior. My gift is life. There has to be a way to bring him back. "He can't die," I insist. "Not yet. Not until I'm old and ugly, and even then, he has to outlive me! Come back. Please."

"Yeh'll never be old or ugly," James rasps. "But you are a little heavy."

I sit upright and lift my arms off his body. I watch,

awestruck, as James shifts from lying in my lap to sitting on his knees. The dark mark around his neck has fades into a light purple and the hole in his shoulder is closed. James coughs and something makes a squeaking sound. He lifts his shirt to look at where Peter stabbed him. The wound is an ugly, bloody mess, but it's not leaking. It's just red, and raw, and angry. "A little help with that would be great, mate."

Emmit steps between Peter and Smee. He places his hands over the hole in James's stomach. Blood stains Emmit's shirt red as James's skin heals. He doesn't fully close the wound because it would transfer to him. Instead, Emmit takes enough so that James's insides aren't at risk of falling out. They both need stitches and possibly a shot of scotch to take the edge off, but they're alive.

"How is this possible?" Aria asks.

Pan extends a hand to help James to his feet. He wobbles but finds his footing a moment later. "Wednesday has the gift of life. She can create it." James glances at the cabin where Mira sleeps. "And return it." He looks at Peter briefly, not an ounce of resentment in his eyes, before finding me again.

"I told yeh, Neverland will give yeh anything yeh want. All you had to do was ask, Sunshine." He touches my cheek and I lean into his hand.

I enjoy the warmth of his touch, but only let myself linger in it for a heartbeat. I look at our crew and the lifeless souls on the deck. Our people have survived with some cuts and bruises, but overall, they seem okay. The same can't be said for Belle's soldiers. "Can I save them?"

Emmit presses his lips into a tight line and shakes his head. "You could try, but their souls left their bodies a long time ago. Might be best to let them rest."

"What now?" Smee asks. She hugs herself, out of place as she's the only one of us besides Pan not covered in blood.

"Yeh betrayed me," James says, his voice cold and emotionless.

"I know, and I'm sorry." Smee hangs her head low. I can feel the shame rolling off of her as well as the resentment being shot at her from the crew. It seems as if Neverland hasn't just given me the gift of life, but also made me an empath. The Lost's emotions are waves of color. Blue for sorrow. Purple for resentment. Whereas Smee's are black with fear, orange with desperation, and a smidge of white. Hope.

"Sorry is not enough, Smee. Yeh need to earn my trust back."

"How? I'll do anything," she begs and that orange aura around her burns brighter.

James grunts, but I can see this is all an act. He does not hate Smee or even resent her for her actions. He feels sorrow but he's also hopeful. "For starters, you can help clean the mess you made. Each body deserves a burial."

"I'll help," Xyris says, stepping forward. "I dug graves before I died. Been a long time since I've worked a shovel, but I'm happy to lend a hand."

"I will, too, but I'd like to handle the burning of Belle. Her soul will be tortured if it's not burned to ashes... and I'd like to reclaim my father's old castle." Emmit looks at me. "If that's okay with you."

Belle could use a heavy dose of torment considering all the suffering she's caused, but I agree. Who am I to dictate what Emmit does with the remains of his last family member? So long as she can't come back to life or haunt me, I don't care what he does with her. Or the castle.

"That home belongs to your family. I don't want it. Although, I'd love to peruse the library if you're willing to teach me your language. I'm a sucker for a good book."

"My home is yours, your majesty. You are welcome any time." He bows.

"Don't say that. It's creepy." I'm about to add that he should not bow either when Mira cries from within James's quarters. Like a true princess, she's avoided all the drama and decided it was time for everyone to focus on her. Warmth blooms in my chest at the thought of finally settling down and enjoying these moments with her.

"I'll fetch her," Peter says, a step ahead of Pan as they both race back to the captain's quarters. "She's probably hungry."

James chuckles and watches his brothers leave with a far-off look. "He was always good with the kids."

I nod because Peter is good with Mira. He and Pan both are.

I walk to the side of the ship and lean against the taffrail facing the ocean. I can't look at Neverland, not when she's given me an impossible decision to make. Do I go home to the family I left behind, or do I stay here with the family I chose?

"We can set sail at sunrise...if that's what yeh want," James says, coming up beside me. "I'll need help with steering the ship through the mouth of hell again, but I promise I'll get yeh back to yehr sister.

"No," I say resoundingly. "This is my home now. I worked so hard to be here again, I'm not ready to leave yet."

"Then what seems to be the problem?"

I stare at my hands because looking at him is too difficult. I don't know how I'm going to give any of them up. I don't know if what I'm feeling is love, but the thought of having to let go of him, or Peter, or Pan kills me. "I don't want to say goodbye."

"Why would you say goodbye?" Peter asks, holding Mira in his arms. He's fashioned a makeshift bottle out of a teapot and while it looks absurd, Mira is drinking from it. He whistles once, catching Pan's attention, who comes over to join the conversation.

I turn and lean against the railing to face my boys. The asshole who took my heart without asking. The dark knight who's had my back from day one. And the savior who brought me to life again. How can I let one go and not the others? How can I choose which of them deserves my heart the most? I can't. But I can't string them along either. "It's not right for me to be with all of you."

"Why not?" Pan asks. "I'd rather have some of your time than none of it."

"Same," Peter adds. "I told you before, I won't make you choose and I stand by my word."

"Wendy married me and, eventually, loved me, but she was never truly satisfied. Her heart beat for me but bled for Peter," James says. "I won't be the cause of yehr pain. Love one of us or all of us. The choice is yehrs."

"You don't mean those things," I say, because they can't. They don't know what they're signing up for. Hell, I don't know what they're signing up for. I've never had someone love me enough to put their needs aside and think of me first. I've always been the second choice or an afterthought. And now I have three men willing to do whatever it takes to be with me. "This is crazy."

"No." Pan takes my face in his hand. "This is love. We love you enough to share you with not just each other but with Neverland." He kisses my forehead and then looks down at me. "Besides, who better to teach you how to rule Neverland than me? I am her shadow."

"Was her shadow," Peter interjects. "And what about me? I built every tree house. Are you going to show her how our plumbing system works?"

"Hey now! Who rescued souls and created the cove?" James says.

"Rescued?" Peter guffaws. He glances at Pan, having a conversation only they hear, before turning his back to James.

The boys walk toward the dock together, bickering the way siblings do—about nothing and everything all at once—and my heart is full.

The End.

Sign up for my newsletter to read an exclusive subscriber epilogue featuring a MMMF scene you didn't know you needed in your life.

JOIN MY NEWSLETTER

FOR WEEKLY UPDATES ON ALL THINGS BOOKS AND BAILEY PLUS RECEIVE AN EXCLUSIVE SHOP DISCOUNT

Want another Bailey Black Fantasy Adventure? Turn the page to learn about her other novels.

Looking for some love in your life? Bailey's contemporary romances range from sweet to spicy, with everything in between.

Fake dating, Forced proximity, Office sleepovers, Ex drama, Slow burn tension, He's a little grumpy. She's a little unhinged. And together? Sparks.

Emma Evans had the perfect wedding planned—until her fiancé dumped her a week before the big day. Now she's heartbroken, homeless, and stuck with a non-refundable, high-end wedding package she can't return... or use.

So she does the unthinkable: gives the whole thing away in a viral giveaway.

What she doesn't expect...The winning groom is best friends with her frustratingly attractive landlord, Matthew Anderson. The same man who catches her illegally crashing in her office with a bottle of wine and a Taylor Swift playlist.

Matt has every reason to evict her. Instead, he makes her a deal: fake date him to help sell the love story, and he'll look the other way. It's outrageous. It's risky. But if pretending to be in love for one week keeps her business afloat, Emma's in.

Only, somewhere between staged kisses, scorching chemistry, and one very real wedding, the line between make-believe and something more starts to blur.

And Emma's about to find out that the best love stories never go according to plan.

Enemies to Lovers, High School Bully, Athlete Antihero, First Love, Girl Next Door, Completed Duet

BOOK 1 IN THE BROKEN LOVE SERIES

Piper

Most people don't think about the day they'll die. They coast through life, blissfully unaware of how their time is ticking away. I wasn't like most people. I welcomed death, wanted her to take me away from the prison I called life, but she refused. I tried twice only to survive. And then, when I thought I had nothing left it came.A reason to live.Rex was a small, unexpected ray of light my world of darkness that blossomed into a beam of sunshine. I thought, maybe this was why Death didn't take me. Maybe she knew that if I held on a little longer things would turn around. But the third time Death came to my door wasn't by choice. Someone else brought her, and I fear this time she might take me.

Rex

Being the son of a country star sucks. My parents are never around, I move every year or so, and I have no real friends. Everyone around me has an agenda. Everyone except Piper Lovelace. I can't get that girl to notice me. Trust me I've tried. Thankfully, fate stepped in and gave me the break I needed. I've got her attention, now I need her to give me a chance.

Enemies to Lovers, High School Bully, Athlete Antihero, First Love, Girl Next Door, Completed Duet

BOOK 2 IN THE BROKEN LOVE SERIES

She's beautiful. Fierce. Nothing at all like the girl I used to know, which is absolutely terrifying because Danika Winters is the only person outside of that room who knows the truth. She could ruin me, and I'm not talking about my reputation. I couldn't give two shits about what the kids at St. A's think. I'm talking major, life-altering, jail time ruined. I'll do whatever it takes to keep her quiet. Even if it means destroying the only person I've ever cared about.

Fall In love with a
Bailey Black Book Here

Frienemies to lovers, Fake dating, High school romance, Love triangle

Asher Anderson is a dick.

We aren't friends, so when he seeks me out in the cafeteria on the worst day of my life, I'm suspicious. When he tells Liam Heiter that we're dating, which couldn't be farther from the truth, I want to kill him...Until I see Liam's reaction.

Liam—my best friend, the guy who crushed every hope of us *officially* being together—is jealous. He has never looked at me this way and I love it.

So, I play along. Maybe watching me with someone else will make Liam suffer like I have the past four years. And maybe, just maybe, he'll come to his senses and realize we belong together. It's not like I actually *like* Asher. At best, I tolerate him. What's the worst that can happen?

**Fall In love with a
Bailey Black Book Here**

Small town, Opposites attract, Cowboy, New girl in town, Unexpected parenthood (+denial)

Josh

Josh Andrews hadn't expected to meet the girl of his dreams in a church parking lot—especially not while his best friend was hooking up in his truck. But there she was, parked two spaces away, pretending not to notice his predicament. Layla was gorgeous, sharp-witted, and completely immune to his charm. He should have walked away. Instead, he couldn't stop thinking about her. Layla wasn't like the girls who usually fell for his easy smile and smooth lines. She challenged him, saw right through him—and he liked it. For the first time, he wanted more than just a fleeting connection. He wanted her.
Winning her over won't be easy, but Josh has never backed down from a challenge. And Layla? She might just be the one risk worth taking.

**Fall In love with a
Bailey Black Book Here**

Second chance, The dare/bet, Insta chemistry, Learning to love, Shared Pasts

I've sworn off men forever! Okay, not forever, but for a few months. After my last hook-up, my vag needs a reset because the last man to touch me broke it in the worst of ways. Not a problem until my new dance partner comes into the picture. He's turning into my forbidden fruit, tempting me in ways I didn't know possible.

I have three months of celibacy ahead of me and eight weeks to whip my new dance partner into shape.

Someone save me.

Fake dating, Second chance, Friends to lovers, Everybody can see it, Short and Spicy novella

A wedding. A lie. And regret.

I'm in over my head with not one but two ex-boyfriends at the same wedding. Both of which I haven't seen in over a year. When the one who ripped my heart into pieces backs me into a corner, I grab the other and kiss him.

Yup. This is how I ended up fake dating Noah Ruckers, and let me tell you, it's an emotional roller coaster. I thought I'd put my feelings for him behind me. We spent years as friends after our break up, nothing more. But no matter how hard I try I can't forget what his lips feel like. Or the way his arms wrap around me.

In two days, I'm walking away. There is no future for us. But that doesn't mean I can't pretend.

Fall In love with a
Bailey Black Book Here

Fake dating, Second chance, Friends to lovers, Everybody can see it, Short and Spicy novella

Holly Flynn is a leprechaun who grants wishes—but with a dangerous twist. Each wish comes at a price: once it's fulfilled, the "victim" forgets everything before their wish—and her.

When a gorgeous stranger asks for one unforgettable night, things take an unexpected twist. The chemistry between them is electric, and soon, Holly's struck by a terrifying thought: She doesn't want him to forget her.

Then, a week later, he knocks on her door. And he remembers everything.

Why does he remember, when no one else does? Is it fate—or is her magic betraying her?

How About a Fantasy Adventure?

Dive into the completed Neverland Novels. Characters have been aged up for this darker, grittier version. If you like your fairytale retellings with hot, ruthless, morally gray love interests, you'll enjoy this series. The Lost Darling is the first book in the main storyline. Please read this series in order.

Twisted Fairy Tale, Peter Pan Retelling, Multiple Love Interests, Morally Gray Males, She's Mine, Scorching hot lost boys, Spice, and more!

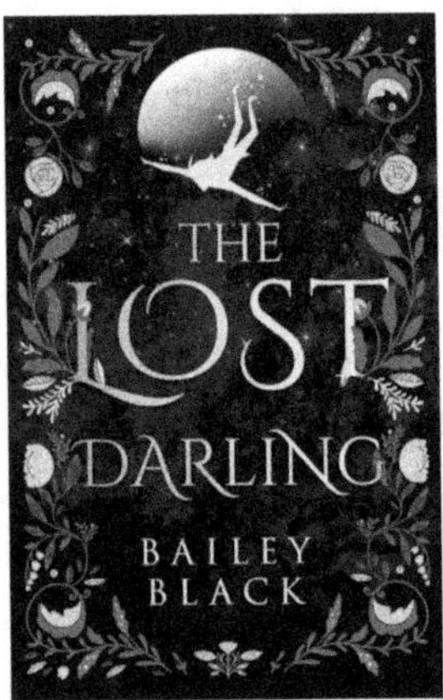

Second star to the left and continue until morning.

I got that line tattooed on my wrist the day I turned twenty-one. So much symbolism in such a simple sentence. At the time, it was a nod to the future and the infinite possibilities to come, while reminding me to remember the past and to look for magic in the world.

Growing up, nothing was ever what it seemed. The shift of leaves on a tree was a Faery skipping by. Shooting stars were a chance to make wishes. Shadows were souls stuck between this world and the next, mirroring a life they once had.

My imagination was limitless, the world a wonderful adventure waiting to unfold.

It's easy to lose that sense of wonder with the weight of life on your shoulders and I wanted a reminder to get me through the hard days.

Most importantly, it was an ode to the boy who earned the title of my first crush, even if he was animated. Peter Pan wasn't a *save the damsel* kind of prince. He was daring, and selfless, and took care of the ones he loved. He was a friend to all but never afraid to fight the Pirates when their moral compass broke. Wendy was an idiot for leaving him. She rushed home to a heartless world full of men willing to lie through their teeth to get down her pants.

But that's the beauty of a book, the characters are perfectly flawed. Damaged just enough that we still love them. Whereas reality is nothing but empty promises and baggage the size of mountains.

The day I got my tattoo, I would have given anything to be whisked away into a fairytale. My world was crumbling, and all I wanted was to go back to when life was simpler. I didn't realize I had sealed my fate in ink.

Branded myself as one of the Lost.

Neverland was everything the stories made it out to be. Beautiful. Full of magic. Filled with handsome men and debonair pirates. But the author of my favorite tale left out one crucial detail.

In order to get there, you have to die.

A witch in a world where magic is illegal, A revenge mission, A rescue mission, Death. People die. Sorry, not sorry, 2 love interests (not a RH and not a triangle), A touch of enemies to lovers. He falls first she falls harder

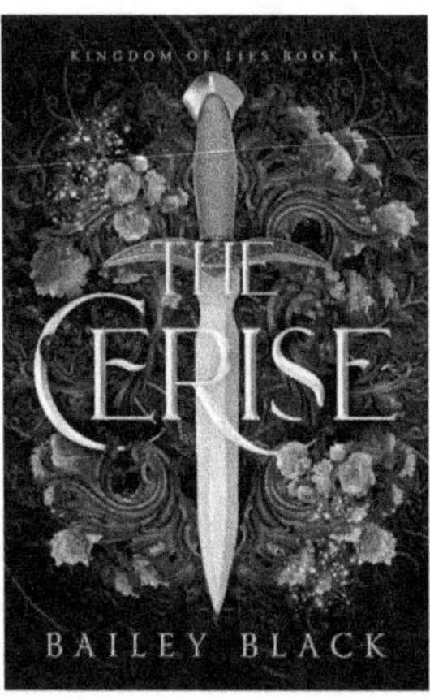

I had a plan. Find the soldier who killed my family and make him pay. It should have been an easy feat. I'd done it over a dozen times, taking out each member of that regiment one by one, but the mission went sideways. It all started with the man in the woods. The one my webs of magic couldn't sense even when he stood before me. Then my partner made a mistake, and now he's lying in one of the Crown's dungeons, fighting for his life. I couldn't leave him to die, but I couldn't just walk into the castle either.

Or maybe I could.

With the help of some unexpected allies, I entered the Culling—a one-in-a-lifetime chance to become queen. I have no interest in winning the prince's heart, or the crown. My only goal is to get into the castle, find my friend, and get out before someone realizes I'm a Cerise.

But when the welcome ball turns from a grand event into a nightmarish dance of death, all eyes are on me. As if that's not bad enough, the soldier, the one who took my family, he's here.

If you loved "The Selection" by Kiera Cass and "From Blood and Ash" by Jennifer L. Armentrout, get ready to fall in love with this enchanting fantasy romance!

Sometimes I think the Thank You section is the saddest part of the whole story because it means it's over.

A special thank you to Heather Douglas for being my star beta reader. All of the beautiful quotes on IOTL's graphics are all because of her.

Thank you to Ashleigh Blakely for being my final set of eyes before publication. Her attention to detail is immaculate.

To my editor Beth at Magnolia Author Services, I don't even know how many books we've worked together on at this point but as long as you want me I will forever be a repeat customer. (Indie authors...if you're looking she's the shit!)

To my husband who says he wants nothing to do with my books but hounds me when I haven't written anything in a week... I love you.

To the bloggers and bookstagrammers who bring my stories to the world. You are amazing! I cannot begin to express how grateful to you I am.

Finally, I'd like to thank my readers. Every time you open one of my books, you make my dream come true.

Thank you.

Xoxo

Bailey

I've always wanted to be a writer. I remember my first time really trying to write. It was after I saw Practical Magic and I knew there was more to those characters. Being the creative ten-year-old I was, I managed to write a solid two paragraphs on my mother's dinosaur of a laptop. Fast forward fifteen years, when I was a new stay-at-home mom with no time for friends, let alone a life. I rediscovered my love for reading, which turned into a love of writing. There were A LOT of bad stories in the beginning (those aren't published) but I eventually honed my craft and grew brave enough to publish them in the world.

I'm not a full-time author as of yet. I'm still a mom and a wife and somehow balancing a job along with all the responsibilities tied to adulthood. My writing hours are slim, but man when I dive into a world it's hard to get me out of it.

So far, I've been lucky enough to have readers just as enamored with my characters as I am. It still humbles me that there are readers and bloggers out there willing to take a chance on my stories. So while this is a little bit about me, it's also about you because without your support I wouldn't have a career.

Thank you, from the bottom of my heart, for always believing on me.

@baileysbookbesties

@baileysbookbesties

@baileysbookbesties